HADES

GUARDIANS

VALERIE TWOMBLY

Copyright © 2019 by Valerie Twombly

Editing by: JRT Editing & The Writing Hall

Cover by: Original Syn

All rights reserved.

No part of this book may be reproduced in any form or by any electronic or mechanical means, including information storage and retrieval systems, without written permission from the author, except for the use of brief quotations in a book review.

ISBN: 978-1-7326306-8-0

Print ISBN: 978-1-5323-9889-6

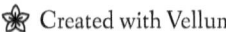 Created with Vellum

DEDICATION

For my fans. You have waited a long time for this story and I am so excited to be able to finally bring it to you.

INTRODUCTION

Being the lord of dark, terrifying things makes Hades the most feared god in existence. He's also the most bored. When the guardians request his assistance, he is quick to grant it and make his way to the human realm. After all, creating havoc is what he does best. When his path crosses with a beautiful female, he finds her honesty refreshing, making his desire burn hotter. It's when she summons him for a favor that he will finally get to name his terms.

When tall, dark and oh-so-sexy walks into her store, Mia suddenly finds herself marked by a god. Saddled with a curse that rips her world apart on a nightly basis, she decides bargaining with Hades to remove it might prove beneficial. Of course, requesting a favor from the lord of the Underworld comes with a huge price. Namely thirty days in Hell as his guest.

Hades is only out for some fun, but Mia isn't playing his games. She intends to get through her agreement despite the yearning she feels for him. Problem is, the longer they are together the more she begins to see beyond the lord of evil to the troubled man beneath. Now she must decide if he is worthy of the only thing she has left to give.

CHAPTER ONE

HADES DRILLED an intense glare into his latest victim. The man, who had been a child molester in his human life wore a smirk across his mouth as he looked up at Hades from where he knelt. The god of the Underworld intended to wipe that smile off the bastard personally. With his boot.

"Do you know where you are?" Hades asked, not really giving a shit if the man did or not. He was bored with torturing these days and contemplated new ways to make the afterlife an eternal hell.

The man shrugged. "You're definitely not god. Maybe his lackey?"

Hades never flinched at the insult. He had certainly been accused of many things. All of which were mostly true, but he was a god. The god of dark, terrifying torture. He flicked his wrist and the man was instantly naked. His genitalia forever changed by Hades' hand into that of a female. The man looked down and screamed.

"What the fuck?" He cupped where his junk had once been. "Fix me!"

Hades yawned. "Your howling bores me. Since you liked playing games with little girls, I thought you might enjoy becoming one." He leaned closer. "Hundreds of demons will enjoy fucking you to death." He laughed. "Oh, wait. My bad, you're already dead."

He snapped his fingers and four demons appeared. "Remove this filth from my sight." His minions quickly grabbed arms and legs and dragged the screaming condemned from the room. With that out of the way, he summoned one of the many succubi that resided in the palace. Aster appeared, her thick locks of raven hair caressed naked hips as she moved to him, a crystal goblet in hand. Stopping before him, she offered the glass. "My lord, how may I please you?" She licked her lips, green eyes flashing, and her desire thickened the air.

He accepted the glass and sipped the burgundy liquid. "Be creative. I'm bored." He eased onto his throne. When she reached for him, he moved her hand away. "Dance for me."

"Yes, my lord." She began a slow seductive sway, and Hades wondered what was wrong in his world that his cock didn't even stir. Perhaps it was the fact he saw the truth inside every living soul. He was privy to their weaknesses, their desires, and the darkness so many sought to hide. He saw through it all. The demon who danced for him hoped to gain favor and power by giving Hades what she thought he wanted.

Hell, not even he knew anymore what he truly desired. His mind was so numb and his body unresponsive to everything around him. The Underworld had become his own eternal hell. As he watched Aster dance, he tried not to fall asleep. The markings on his right forearm tingled once more, indicating another fucked-up soul had entered Hell. Each time a person was condemned, his power grew. The only thing that kept him in check was to transfer some of his energy to his army. Just enough to keep his demons powerful, yet not even they were able to best him. He doubted that even his eldest brother, Zarek, the king who presided over them all held more power.

Soon, he would be able to find out. His time here was ticking. One way or another, he was getting free of his prison.

MIA WALKED DOWN THE SIDEWALK, having left early enough so she had time to stop along the way and help those less fortunate. New Orleans wasn't unlike many of the cities across the U.S., according to the news. Buildings were covered with soot from the fires that burned continually, and the sky was filled with grayish-black smoke. She wondered how they had ended up with demons destroying their world. The obvious answer was everyone had lost faith, and this was humanity's punishment.

Some demigod calling himself Lowan, along with his minion demons, torched everything in sight as a way of punishing the humans who chose not to follow him. Or in some cases, humanity itself did the burning so there was nothing left for the demons to take.

The world was bleak.

Tucking her basket closer she continued her journey, intent on helping someone. As she rounded the corner, she spotted a woman with two small children huddled together on the sidewalk against an abandoned building. With the sun filtering through the thick mass of smoke, the demons were not likely to be out, but she laid her palm on the knife tucked in her pocket anyway.

"Hello." She made sure her voice carried over the breeze yet remained gentle.

The woman looked up, her eyes filled with fear and sorrow and it tugged at Mia's heart. The woman remained quiet and pulled her children closer. Mia knelt so she was on the same level.

"I have food and blankets." She set the basket down and pushed it toward the woman. "Please take it." Mia didn't have much, but she would share what little she did.

The woman's gaze darted to the other buildings as if she feared the darkness would snake out and snatch her prize away.

"The demons are not likely to come into the daylight." It was something she had learned the hard way when wandering into an abandoned building.

The woman reached for the basket and it was then Mia saw her twisted arm. The lady shook her head. "Not them. The others who live here."

Mia looked around but didn't see anyone; however, she sensed they were being watched. "What happened to your arm?"

While the woman pulled food from the basket and handed it to her daughters, she gave Mia a quick, tear-filled glance. "I was only trying to feed my girls when one of the men guarding the buildings refused to let me in. My arm was broken in the scuffle."

Her anger flared. The war with the demons had succeeded in bringing the worst out of most, and she was simply done with it. "I wish I could do more, but this is all I have."

"I can mend her," a soft voice spoke from behind Mia. She rose and whipped around to face a beautiful woman with intense green eyes.

"I've seen you somewhere."

"My name is Cassie. I've been to New Orleans a few times."

Mia searched her memories. "No. I think it was on the news or something." She would never forget eyes that color.

The female moved closer. "Yes, I'm one of the guardians. I used to be human before I mated with Marcus."

Mia stepped in front of the injured woman and her children. How she intended to protect them against the female in front of her, she hadn't a clue.

"I'm a healer. I can fix her arm."

Mia glanced behind her and gave the other woman a questioning look.

"I trust her. I've seen her around doing god's work," the woman replied.

"Fine." She stepped aside.

Cassie knelt and touched the deformed arm. A white light encompassed the injured woman. "What is your name?" Cassie asked.

"Marion. Thank you."

"You're welcome." When the guardian finished, she rose, and Marion's arm appeared normal.

"Wow. That's amazing." A sudden idea came to Mia. "Can you cure me?"

Cassie looked at her, a frown on her face. "I need to touch you to see what your ailment is."

Mia swallowed shame then nodded. Cassie laid a gentle hand on Mia's arm and closed her eyes. Several minutes ticked by before she opened them again and spoke.

"I'm afraid I can't help. I am so sorry."

Mia batted away unshed tears. "It's okay. I didn't think there was anything you could do. Maybe you can help make these demons go away?"

Cassie stared into the distance before she brought her focus back to Mia. "What is your name?"

"Mia."

A sad smile creased her mouth. "Mia. I wish I could make all of this go away, but it seems we are at the mercy of something bigger than us." A fiery spark ignited the green in her eyes. "However, I have a plan that might at least give all of us a reprieve."

LILETA FLARED out her power and summoned a portal that carried her to Katie's home. She placed a platter of finger sandwiches on the kitchen table. "Ladies, we have turkey with swiss and ham with cheddar."

"I. Am. Starved." Katie grabbed two sandwiches and practically inhaled them.

Cassie laughed. "Of course, you are. You're not carrying any ordinary baby. I know when I was pregnant, I thought I would starve to death." She stirred the pitcher of lemonade Katie shoved in front of her. "I was constantly sending Marcus out in the middle of the night for all kinds of crazy concoctions."

Ranata stepped up with a cake that seriously looked like death by chocolate. "I can't wait for Baal and me to have kids, but I've got way too much on my plate right now to even think about it." She set the platter holding the round perfection that was coated in dark frosting and decorated with chocolate shavings on the table. With a sly grin, she looked up. "You can't have a baby shower without chocolate."

"You have just become our bestest friend," Lileta laughed. "I'm so happy we could get together for this. But where's Gwen?"

"She couldn't get away but sent a gift," Cassie responded.

The girls filled their plates and headed to the patio. "I feel guilty sitting here with the sun on my face eating all this wonderful food," Katie replied, rubbing her large belly. "I could be helping, but Seth insists I stay here."

"Our mates can be overbearing at times." Ranata chuckled. "Try being mated to a demon." All the women nodded in agreement.

"All of us have certainly had some adjustments to this life." Cassie picked at her bread crust.

"You were the first. Right?" Ranata asked.

Cassie laughed. "Yeah. I remember the first time I saw Marcus. I nearly fainted." Her cheeks flushed. "I never told you this, but I had dreams. Very sensual dreams and when I actually met the man in person..." She shook her head. "Later I found out he wasn't who I thought, but so much more."

"How did you take it when you found out?" Katie asked.

"I freaked the hell out and told him I never wanted to see him again." She played with her napkin. "It was Aidyn who told me I was pregnant, and Marcus had gone missing. The fear in his voice convinced me I needed to help." She shrugged. "And here we are now. I mated a vampire and now I'm a guardian."

Lileta stared at her cake. "I knew Caleb was different when he rescued me first from Odage and later from Lowan."

"At least you had the benefit of being a demon and knowing immortals existed," Cassie pointed out.

"True. But our species—a dragon and a demon—were never

meant to be together, and I fought it for as long as I could." Her smile turned wistful. "He taught me to trust again."

"I always knew I was different." Katie flashed a nervous glance at Lileta. "I feel like I should apologize. I had no idea there were good demons when I was busy killing them."

Lileta leaned over, her jet-black hair falling forward when she patted Katie on the arm. "It's okay. Your own story is crazy."

Katie laughed, her emerald eyes flashing. "Boy, you're not kidding. To find out my mate was the first guardian created and was on a fast train to nutsville. Top that with discovering my real father was the Phoenix god and I went from human to goddess in a burst of flames? Nope, just another day for me."

The girls laughed.

"Katie, you were a wise choice for Seth and I'm so glad he found you. I don't think anyone else could have saved him," Cassie said.

The goddess winked at her. "I've always been a ball of fire."

Laughter echoed across the patio again.

Lileta turned to the newest member. "Ranata. You're the newbie and I'm so proud to call you sister."

The woman flashed a bright smile. "I thought my story was strange, but after getting to know you ladies... Not so much."

"Oh, I don't know. You found out you were not only half fae but now their queen." Cassie tipped her head. "Your Highness."

Ranata rolled her blue eyes. "Stop."

"How is that whole thing going anyway?" Katie asked. "Will your people be joining the fight?"

"Soon. My warriors are preparing."

Silence fell with the talk of war and they went back to stuffing their faces. Several minutes passed, with only the songs of the birds breaking the silence, before Lileta finally decided it was now or never to reveal the plan she and Cassie had hashed out.

"I have an idea I wanted to present to you guys. It's kinda farfetched, but... I think we can make it happen." She set her plate aside and prepared herself for any rebuttals she might receive. She looked to each woman in front of her and knew that every one of them had faced their own inner battle when they realized they were fated to spend eternity with an immortal. Life for them had changed in so many ways.

"Cassie and I want to have Christmas." There, she blurted it out but now it needed a follow up with an explanation.

Cassie jumped in. "We don't mean only us. We mean there has to be a way to give the people at least a day of peace. Let them celebrate however they wish but without the worry of demon attacks." Cassie took a slow breath. Obvious tears threatened to spill. Lileta knew that every day Cassie cried for the children. The guardian had spent too many years as a nurse watching terminally ill kids either fight and live, or fight and lose the battle not to have this weigh on her too.

"I love the idea, but how are we supposed to stop a war?" Ranata whispered.

"Katie, you're a goddess. Maybe you can talk to Zarek and convince him to stop this?" Cassie pleaded. Perhaps the god could be convinced.

The redhead rubbed her belly. "I fucking love your idea, but Zarek forbids any interference. He would lock us all up until his temper tantrum was over, which for him could be centuries."

Cassie sighed. "I refuse to give up. We need to show the human race some kind of hope. I mean, they still don't trust us and how can we ask them to fight if we don't give them something in return?"

Aidyn, the guardian king had recently gone public with the existence of the guardians. Not exactly what people had considered the angelic beings that protected their world to look like. Instead, they ended up with a race of ancients with fangs who drank blood for strength. Aidyn hadn't dared let on about the others. Demons who were friends, dragons that shifted into humans, and fae? The world wasn't ready for that yet. Hell, they weren't ready to place their faith in the guardians. At least not until Lowan was dead.

Lileta cleared her throat. "Ladies. I happen to know a certain someone who is powerful and thinks I'm the best thing since canned ham." She waved her hand. "Or whatever."

"Lileta, while I'm sure your mate would be more than happy to kill Lowan on the spot.

"I wasn't referring to Baal," Lileta stated.

"Then who?" Katie asked. All the women stared at Lileta, willing the answer to pass her lips.

"Hades."

"But he's a god and therefore follows their stupid rules." Cassie flashed a quick glance at Katie. "No offense."

"None taken."

"It's not like we're asking him to kill Lowan, only make him cease for a day. It doesn't hurt to ask, and I don't mind." Lileta pushed her raven hair from her face. "Hell, I bet he would even come here, and if we plead our case together, he might be happy to defy the others."

Katie's face paled. "Come here? Can he do that?"

The god of the Underworld had never been known to leave his realm.

"We could go to him. That might actually be better anyway. Zarek would be less likely to find out and try to stop us," Lileta said.

"Our mates will be sorely pissed." Ranata grinned.

"Let's go," Cassie said, determination filled her voice.

Lileta set down her glass. "I'm in. I say we go now." Then looked to Katie who tossed aside a napkin.

"Well, count me in. I'm bored sitting around here anyway." Katie pushed herself up belly first. "Besides, I've never been to Hell. Could be fun and I'd get to meet my uncle." She let out a hysterical laugh. "I'm fucking related to Hades. How unreal is that shit?"

Lileta sucked in a breath. Her nerves were a little tight. After all, while Hades was her god, she wasn't sure how he'd take the four of them popping in unannounced. Not to mention what they were about to request him to do. Granted, he loved breaking rules, but he was also about what he'd get out of the deal. Perhaps being his great-granddaughter would hold some weight.

"I have to admit, I've never met Hades," Cassie stated.

Lileta reached out. "Everyone hold hands." Once they were linked, she flashed them to the Underworld where they appeared directly in Hades' main living area. The god was busy nuzzling the neck of a female. One hand held a glass of wine, the other was firmly wrapped around her breast. He raised his head, apparently sensing the intrusion.

"Who the fuck dare disturb me?" he growled.

"Shit. You didn't mention he was hotter than sin," Katie blurted out.

"Eww. Seriously? You two are related." Cassie wrinkled her nose.

Lileta groaned at the goddess tact or lack thereof. Sure, Hades was dressed in black leather pants, a white tee stretched tight across his broad chest and biker boots. His raven hair fell loose past his shoulders and a shadow darkened his jaw. Black glyphs marked his right forearm and appeared to pulse. While all the gods were pleasant to look at, Hades was exceptional. He was dark and dangerous. A predator no one wished to mess with. Even the evilest of evil dared not cross him.

CHAPTER TWO

LIFTING A BROW, Hades straightened and looked at the women. "Well, what do we have here? Lileta? Care to explain, love?"

Lileta stepped forward. "We came to ask a favor." She gave a slight bow.

"I see. Interesting." He glanced back at the demon who he'd been fondling, not really in the mood for fucking anyway. "Leave us."

She pushed out her bottom lip but obeyed and vanished into thin air. Hades sauntered closer to the ladies. He brought the glass to his lips and sipped while he stared at them over the rim.

"My lord, you know Ranata, but this is Cassie and Katie." Lileta kept her chin up and her gaze locked on his.

He surveyed the women, moving from one to the other until he landed on Katie's rather large belly before he looked up and met her gaze. "Daughter of the Phoenix. I wondered when we would finally meet." He gave a nod toward her stomach. "I see you've been busy."

She lifted a shoulder then responded, "What can I say, my mate is killer in the sack."

He threw his head back and deep laughter filled the room. "I like a girl with spunk. If you ever tire of your life in Zarek's world be sure to let me know. I could use someone like you down here."

"I'll keep that in mind."

"Ladies, please have a seat." He snapped his fingers and several leather chairs appeared in front of the hearth where four-foot flames crackled. He gestured and Ranata led the way. A tray of refreshments appeared on the coffee table between the seats.

"Help yourselves." He summoned his throne and noted Lileta rolling her eyes.

"Are those demon skulls?" Cassie pointed at the arms of his chair.

He grinned as he petted one. "It never pays to piss me off." He shrugged. "Unless of course you wish to become part of my furnishings. Now, to what do I owe having such beauties pay me a visit?" Leaning forward, he said, "Do your mates know you are here?"

"Hell, no." Cassie shook her head. "Otherwise, we would have never been allowed to come."

"We want to stop the fighting for the holidays," Lileta blurted out.

"Interesting. Continue."

"We thought it would be nice to give the children Christmas. A day of peace could go a long way in building trust in the world," Cassie jumped in.

He steepled his fingers against his lips and contemplated his next words. "You do realize Christmas is a bullshit holiday and not celebrated by the entire human race?"

"We don't have to refer to it as Christmas. It's a holiday of peace, but first we need you to stop the fighting." Cassie relaxed into her seat.

"Ahh, there it is." Hades shifted and tapped his fingers on a skull that looked like it had belonged to a deformed crocodile. "I'm pretty sure you're aware of the rules where the gods are not to interfere? This also includes killing my grandson, Lowan, or do I need to explain it to you?"

Katie attempted to cross her legs, but her belly made it impossible. Instead she wiggled herself to the edge of her seat. "Look, asshat. We're well aware of the fucking rules, but you strike me as a man who likes to not only bend them but snap them in half. Let's face it, you thrive on chaos."

Hades leaned closer to Katie and studied her until finally his mouth twitched. He waved his hand. "There are some rules even I won't break."

"You are seriously going to back down and let the other gods bully you?" Katie raised a delicate brow.

Hades checked his temper. Barely. "So, daughter of the Phoenix. I can assume then you're willing to help? Break the rules, I mean? After all, you have power in your own right. Shall we simply say fuck fate and kill Lowan now?"

"We're not asking you to kill him," Ranata spoke up.

He focused his gaze on the fae queen. "You're not? Then what, exactly, are you expecting me to do?" He leaned back, folded his arms, and waited for a response.

"Since all demons fall under your jurisdiction, we were hoping you could call them off for a day or two. Without them to do his bidding, Lowan might be forced to retreat," Lileta replied. The others nodded their heads in agreement.

"I see. So, have you considered the havoc a demigod might create when he throws his temper tantrum because his minions have been taken away?" He sipped his wine and waited for an answer which never came. The girls just exchanged glances.

"Of course not, which means you probably haven't thought about how the humans will react when the fighting stops then restarts again with renewed vigor. They will wonder why you have the power for a temporary truce but not a complete stop to the madness."

"Do you have to be so logical?" Katie asked.

He fought to keep from rolling his eyes. "Seems someone has to."

Cassie sighed. "I refuse to believe there is no hope. Humanity needs this even if it's for a day. They need to believe there is hope."

This time Hades sighed. "I can contain Lowan's army and even

Lowan himself. I'm bored down here anyway and pissing off Zarek has always been a favorite pastime of mine." He leaned forward. "Here's what I'll do for you. Next week is Christmas eve. When the sun finishes rising across the United States on December 24th, I'll hold the peace until midnight on Christmas day. Your humans have less than forty-eight hours of joy to the fucking world, but after that it's back to your regularly scheduled programming of gloom and doom."

"But the holiday will be over in other parts of the world already," Katie stated.

Hades allowed his eyes to glow red. "Take it or not. I don't fucking care."

Cassie squealed and jumped from her seat. "We'll take it. I'll ask Aidyn to make an announcement."

"There are a few requirements in order for this to happen," Hades responded, squashing their ecstatic vibe in the room.

"Here we go," Katie snorted. Lileta gave her the side-eye.

"My name does not get mentioned in public. How would it look if the ruler of Hell performed a good deed?"

Cassie was quick to nod. "No problem."

"Next, someone needs to keep an eye on this hellhole while I'm gone."

The girls exchanged glances. "What exactly do we need to do?" Lileta asked.

Hades shrugged. "You know. The usual shit, like don't let the mice play while daddy's away."

"We will all pitch in," Cassie said.

"Perfect." Hades didn't bother to hide his shit-eating grin. Instead a parchment appeared on the table in front of them. "You will all sign, then we will have a deal."

THE GIRLS SAT around the ten-foot oak conference table at the command center that was tucked deep in the Carpathian Mountains. To say Lileta was nervous was a severe understatement. She'd asked Aidyn to call the meeting with the others because she had something to share. Almost everyone was there except for Lucan. The poor man had recently found out his mate was the sister of their mortal enemy, Lowan. How could he be expected to wrap his head around that?

The others, Katie and Seth sat to her right with Ranata and Baal next to them. Cassie and Marcus were on the left with Marcus's sister Gwen beside him. A vacant seat for Lucan and then Caleb and herself. Aidyn was at the head. Guilt slid over Lileta because Gwen hadn't been at the shower and therefore not part of their little scheme. However, the female guardian had been out on a top-secret mission or she would have been at the shower. Lileta would have to remember to corner Gwen later for details.

Lucan finally strode through the door looking like absolute shit. Lileta doubted the vampire had slept in weeks. Maybe even months. This war was taking a toll on all of them.

"Excellent, everyone is here." Aidyn twirled a pen between his fingers. "I called this meeting at the request of Lileta"—all eyes turned to her—"so the floor is yours."

Both her mate, Caleb, and her brother, Baal, gave her a questioning look. Caleb tried to slip into her mind, but she slammed down a barrier which caused his gaze to narrow.

"So. Where to start?"

"Ahem. I just want to say that all of the women here—with the exception of Gwen—were involved and we all agree," Katie stated.

"What the hell did you do?" A chorus of male voices rang out as they all pinned their mates with a lethal glare.

"I approached the girls and told them my wish to have peace for the holidays. I think it will go a long way in giving humanity hope," Cassie blurted out.

"Well, love. That's a noble idea, but you know it's impossible. We are barely keeping our heads above water since we are way outnumbered. Until the Phoenix god rises, we're pretty much screwed," Marcus pointed out.

"I know and maybe by doing this we can gain the trust of the people. You need reinforcements. Maybe this will bring everyone together and Aidyn might get some volunteers. So, we came up with a plan. We asked Hades for help," Cassie replied.

Seth raised a brow. "You mean he was invited to your little soiree, and Zarek didn't zap you all into the next century?"

Cassie fidgeted. "Well..."

"I took everyone to Hades," Lileta quickly confessed.

"What?" Seth and Marcus exploded with expletives. Arguments about how it was dangerous in the Underworld and the women should have never gone there alone came from the two guardians, their alpha male chests puffed out. The only ones who seemed unfazed were Baal, Lucan, and Gwen. Aidyn had a puzzled look on his face but remained quiet.

Cassie and Katie, irritated at being considered weak, let their mates know in no uncertain terms that they were adults with their own powers and what the hell would Hades do to them anyway? They were lucky Katie didn't bring down the ceiling. Being a goddess, she was likely the most powerful one in the room, but ready to give birth at any moment, her powers had gone a bit wonky.

"Enough," Aidyn's tone was low and even, yet rose above the ruckus. Once he had everyone's attention, he began again. "Ladies. I think your hearts are in the right place and agree, humanity needs a break. What did Hades say?"

Everyone took their seats and Lileta spoke up. "He said he would give us nearly forty-eight hours beginning Christmas eve and ending at midnight on Christmas." Shock registered on every face except those who had actually talked to the god.

Aidyn started to smile. "I should have known he would rebel." Then lines of worry creased his forehead. "What did he want in return?"

"He said the four of us have to watch over his realm while he was gone," Cassie replied.

"Hell no!" Marcus's eyes turned the color of molten steel.

"I agree with Marcus." Seth was rather stern. "You're about to give birth, Katie. The last place you need to go into labor is Hell."

Cassie crossed her arms. "I'm not backing down. Besides, it's not like we need to be there the entire time." She glared at her mate. "You keep me locked away with the gods, and I agreed only because of our daughter. However, Qadira loves our little girl and would be happy to watch over her should I need to leave."

"No. I forbid it."

"As do I," Seth agreed.

Yelling ensued, powers flared, and plaster actually fell from the ceiling. Aidyn jumped to his feet.

"Enough!" Banging his fists on the table.

Lileta was pretty new to the scene here and had always seen the guardian king calm and collected. With his fangs descended and his gaze darkened, there was no doubt he'd had enough of the bickering.

"Look. If it will make you feel better, I think Ranata and I can handle babysitting watch," Lileta offered. It did make sense. She was a demon after all and Ranata was Baal's mate. This could work.

Aidyn looked to Baal who shrugged his shoulders. "My mate is capable and I'm pretty sure every demon worldwide knows if they fuck with her, I will kill them." His eyes narrowed. "Slowly. I can keep a demon alive for centuries while I torture the shit out of him."

Aidyn nodded then looked to Caleb.

"Considering my mate is the sister of the most powerful demon in Hades' army, mated to a dragon *and* Hades' own blood, I doubt she's in any danger. Besides, like Baal, I have faith in her abilities."

Marcus shot a glare of daggers at the other two males. "Way to make us look like shit."

Again, Baal shrugged. "You did it to yourself. Cassie is a smart girl. Seth, I can understand. Katie is ready to give birth anytime, but I would have thought you knew better by now than to tell her no."

Marcus let out a low growl and Gwen punched him in the shoulder. "What the hell?" He snarled at his sister.

"Stop being a pain in the ass. It's not like she has to spend the entire time there. If it makes you feel any better, I will go with." Gwen gave her brother her best sisterly glare.

"Oh, my sister and my mate in Hell. Fucking great." He tossed his hands up. "Fine. I can see I will fare no better at this battle than I have with the demons."

Cassie laid a hand on his shoulder. "Thank you. Though, now that your curse is broken, there is nothing to stop you from checking in on us when we are there."

He simply grunted. Lileta hoped he wasn't too mad at Cassie.

"Fine, it's settled." Aidyn sat back in his chair. "I'll let everyone know."

HADES PULLED IN A LONG, deep breath, enjoying the scent of the salt air as the waves crashed along the shore. It was barely sunrise on Christmas Eve and as promised he'd popped into the human realm. Of course, he chose the beach of Emerald Isle, North Carolina as his first stop.

It had been a long time. Way too long in fact since he'd left Hell. Not that he was able to without an invitation, thanks to his brothers. It was one of the stipulations placed upon him when he was given the realm to watch over. Zarek thought Hades might create too much chaos if left to his own devices and his brother was probably right. Hades had a knack for getting into trouble. It kinda came with the territory. If you were going to rule over evil, you had to be worse than your subjects or they would disregard your every command. He had strived to become everyone's worst nightmare and succeeded.

"How the fuck did you get here?"

Ah, there was Zarek. Hades kept his back to the bastard. "Obviously, I was invited."

"Well, no shit. By who?"

"I thought I sensed you here," Argathos spoke.

Hades turned to face the other god. "Shouldn't your visions have told you I was coming?" Argathos was the god of visions and normally knew before anyone else what the future held.

"Perhaps I did." The god's mouth twitched.

"What the hell?" Zarek roared and turned to face Argathos. "My own brother. You should have told me."

This time Hades chuckled. "You always did like to throw a tantrum. Even as a child you were fucking bossy." The four gods had been born only minutes apart. Zarek first, so he had been in line to become king. Pyros, their now dead brother the Phoenix came next, then Hades the middle child, and Argathos the spoiled baby. One might think they should all be quadruplets twins, but nothing was further from the truth. However, there were a few similarities between them. Zarek and Hades shared the same black hair as their father, while Argathos had their mother's much lighter brown locks. Zarek also had their father's scary-ass silver eyes. Thankfully, Hades and Argathos shared their mother's dark chocolate color, though Hades' did tend to turn the color of fire when he was pissed—or being evil—pretty much the same thing.

"I am the oldest, therefore your king once father was gone," Zarek replied.

Hades waved him off. "And you deemed I would be in charge of those who had gone rogue. You convinced me to take over the realm of Hell and oversee the evil dropped there." His anger grew and the waves crashing on the beach became more thunderous. He'd best rein it in or he might create a worldwide catastrophe. Wouldn't that be something? Headlines would read.

Hades saves earth from demons but unleashes the worst tsunami in history, destroying humankind.

It would certainly give the humans something else to think about, but it wasn't his style.

"You were sent there because you have Father's evil streak."

Zarek lifted a heavy shoulder. "Besides, who better to keep evil in line than the most feared god ever?"

Hades rubbed his chin. He rather liked that title. "I've learned to control myself over the centuries." He recalled the first several hundred years when he'd tortured every soul that entered his domain. He'd been pissed at his brother for locking him away, but as time passed, he had realized it was the right decision. Fuck if he would admit it though. If he could make Zarek feel even the slightest bit of guilt, he would. It was how he rolled.

Centuries later, when Hades finally came out of his red haze, he'd reincarnated the souls less evil and trained them for his army. A select few had even been granted some of his power, though none would ever grow more powerful than him. Hades was able to see inside the soul. Find the dark that resided in every living being. Even now as he stared at his brothers, he knew their darkest side. It was likely what scared Zarek most. Hades knew how low his big brother could sink to get what he desired, and if Hades stuck around too long, his own darkness became a magnet and bad shit happened to decent people.

Zarek narrowed his gaze and studied Hades under his imaginary microscope. Several minutes ticked by before he spoke again. "It's not time for you to be here, so who invited you and why?"

Hades might be one bad ass, but he was no snitch. Who knew what Zarek might do to his own. However, Lileta belonged to the demon realm and fell under Hades' domain, as now did Ranata. "Lileta and Ranata came to me requesting a favor. I granted it."

Zarek's chest puffed out as his anger rose.

"Brother, is it too much to ask for a direct answer?" Argathos had always been the voice of reason and Hades' favorite.

"Fine. They wanted peace for Christmas, so I'm here to grant it." He held up his hand. "It's only until midnight tomorrow and I best get to summoning my demons before I am accused of not being a man of my word." He snapped his fingers and vanished. Zarek's anger still surrounded him like a black cloud.

CHAPTER THREE

MIA SLIPPED in the back door of the Mini Mart and shrugged off her coat. She hurried through the store, flipping lights along the way, until she finally made it to the front where she turned the sign to open and unlocked the door. Next, she started stocking shelves and tried not to think about what lurked outside. It was early in the morning and she was a little twitchy. The wind tossed a garbage can across the parking lot and had her reaching for her blade. She rose and peered over the top of the shelf, staring out of the picture windows through the front of the store. While she knew demons were not usually out in the daylight, it didn't mean they had never been seen. However, they seemed to prefer darkness to wield their nightmarish deeds.

The lightening sky revealed nothing out of the ordinary. She laughed. What the hell was ordinary these days anyway? Demons were real and so was some asshole who was in charge of them and wanted humanity to bow to his whim.

Picking up the empty box, Mia pushed a dark curl from her eyes, cursing how she'd been blessed with her mother's unruly hair and would kill for long, straight locks. Even a flat iron wouldn't tame this beast. Heading back to the counter, the bell chimed, indicating a customer had entered. She turned to greet them with a smile, but instead her mouth momentarily dropped open. Staring back at her was the most gorgeous man she'd ever laid eyes on. Silky, black as midnight hair lay perfectly straight past his shoulders. Odd, considering the wind outside. Brown eyes with flecks of copper studied her. If she didn't know better, she would swear fire burned behind them. A firm jaw shadowed by a few days' growth framed the most delectable lips she had ever seen.

"Can I help you?" Lord, how had she managed to find her voice?

"Twizzlers." His reply was low, dark, and sent a shiver up her spine.

"Second aisle." She pointed and watched as he moved quiet and stealthy as a panther. Black leather covered a round ass that looked as if it were chiseled from granite it was so firm.

Damn that be fine.

He stopped midstride and looked over his shoulder at her, a wicked grin curved kissable lips. Panic made her wonder if she had mistakenly spoken out loud. But no, she was certain she hadn't. The TV in the corner shrilled, indicating a broadcast was coming through, so she forced her gaze away from that fine ass to watch the news.

The handsome man they called Aidyn appeared with the woman she'd seen earlier. A child cradled in her arms. Supposedly, they were some kind of guardians or angels, she wasn't sure, but what she did know was the demons were still out there and she was terrified. A strong presence brushed against her, causing her to glance out of the corner of her eye only to find Mr. Hottie had slipped in beside her.

"Do you think these people are who they say? I mean, if they really are angels, then why can't they stop the evil?" she asked her strange customer. Did she really want his opinion or just to hear that sinful voice again?

He stared straight at the screen. "That one is more than anyone realizes."

She faced him straight on. "Huh? What does that mean?"

"Listen."

Mia ripped her focus away from the distraction next to her and back to the broadcast. "Peace? For the holidays?" She laughed. "If they can't stop this Lowan and his army of nasty creatures, how the hell do they expect to make him behave for Christmas?" She marched behind the counter, having enough of false hopes. Mr. Hottie stepped up and placed an entire box of Twizzlers on the counter. She raised a brow.

"Must be your favorite."

"I can't get them where I live."

"Serious? Where you from, outer space?"

He tossed a fifty on the counter. "Not far, yet not close."

Well, that was the strangest damn answer she'd ever heard. Apparently, the guy wanted his privacy. She got that.

VANILLA WAFTED through the room and Hades wanted to bathe in it. He hated vanilla, but the scent was coming from the beauty behind the counter, and he suddenly had an intense craving for it. For her. Granted, the only females he'd been with in centuries were demons. Still, they were the most beautiful in the world. This creature in front of him was different with her swirl of copper curls that reached her shoulders. Stormy gray eyes stared back at him and made him wonder what brewed behind them. He searched deeper into her soul. Used his gift to see her truth and what he found startled him. She was not unlike him. Desires, fears, and her own torture had him pulling away to bring his focus back to her full lips. A mouth he suddenly wanted to plunder, and this new desire unsettled him.

"You would like peace for the holiday?" he questioned, already knowing where she stood on the matter.

"I want peace period, but I highly doubt they are going to bring it."

He tried not to study her, but the sweater she wore didn't do anything to hide her ample breasts. His gaze did a lazy glide downward. Over faded jeans that revealed full, round hips. The woman was all curves, exactly how he liked them. He could have her right here and ease the pressure behind his zipper. There was no missing the fact she was also aroused. Yet... Something held him back. An urge he had never before experienced. He wanted this female but not here. Not like this. A woman like her deserved better, so he ignored his discomfort and continued the conversation. "A little skeptical, are you?"

She rang up his order. "That's nineteen ninety-nine. You want this in a bag?"

"No need. You didn't answer my question." He wasn't sure why, but her opinion was important.

"They haven't fixed it yet. How many people have died or been terrorized?"

He stiffened. "Have you been terrorized?" The thought of her even being looked at by one of Lowan's henchmen iced over his very soul. Never a good thing when you were Hades.

"No, but I feel I've been lucky so far. I try to stay under the radar." She shoved an unruly curl out of the way, and he rolled his fingers to keep from reaching out to do it for her.

He sensed her lying but rather than press the issue, he ignored it. "What is your name?"

"Mia."

"Mia." He liked the way it rolled off his lips. "Hold out your hand." He pushed a slight compulsion at her, so she would comply. Long, delicate fingers tipped with pink polish reached out. He took her hand, not missing the instant warmth that nearly made him shiver. The smoothness of her creamed coffee skin was like heaven against his fingertips. Turning over her hand, he placed two fingers at her wrist then slowly traced across her palm until he reached the tips of her fingers where he lingered for a moment. He was loath to break contact but knew he must.

She blinked, then thick lashes lowered over her stormy eyes. "What was that about?"

He grinned. "You have been marked. You're now under my protection. No demon will dare touch you." And if any did, they would know his full wrath.

Her eyes widened, and she stared at her hand. "What? Who the hell are you?"

"I am the lord of the dark. The one who will silence the evil, so you can have your holiday."

She gasped and backed up. "The devil?"

Her words stung. He slapped his palms down and leaned over the counter. "The devil is a spineless prick who kneels at my feet. I hold more power in my pinky than that bastard does in his entire body. He quivers when I speak his name. I am Hades, god of the Underworld, and I will be back for you." He didn't bother to use the door. Instead, he summoned his power, wanting to show her how strong he was and left in a swirl of black smoke.

MIA STARED at the empty space where the hot number... Umm, Hades—as he had referred to himself—had been standing. Her gaze then quickly went to her hand where he had traced his fingers. Her palm still tingled with heat and it freaked her out. There was nothing there, at least visibly anyway, and that made her heart race even more.

She swallowed.

He said he would be back for her. "What the hell does that even mean?" she yelled at no one, and thank god, because she didn't want an answer. "And why the hell am I attracted to the fucking devil?" Oh wait. Not the devil but Hades, as if there was a damn difference. She forced her shaky legs to carry her to the coffee machine and poured herself a mocha. She needed to think and began to pace. Her hands trembled so badly she left a trail of coffee in her wake. This had to be some kind of sick joke. She stopped and forced her shoulders to relax.

"Yeah, a joke." She sipped her beverage then suddenly remembered he had vanished into thin air. "Okay, not a joke." Pushing back an aggravating curl, she went back to the counter and sat on a stool. Hopefully, some customers would come in soon and take her mind off the morning's crazy events. The silence in the room was deafening, and since radio no longer worked, she stuck her iPod into the slot on her speaker box and turned on some soothing music.

The door jangled, and a middle-aged lady stuck her head in. "You have to come see this."

Mia shoved off her stool. "What's going on?" She headed for the door and stepped into the crisp air. The sun making its way higher into the sky took the edge off the cool breeze.

"It's true." A man shouted as he ran by.

Mia walked to the sidewalk where the woman stood and looked down the street. "What's..." Her jaw dropped, and she instinctively shoved her hand over her gaping mouth. Standing in the middle of the street was Mr. Sexy himself. His face turned to the sky and his hands outstretched. Wind whipped around him, but his hair never moved. Screams laced with pain filled the morning air and she had to cover her ears. Hades, or whoever he was, snapped his gaze back to the street and started walking, shouting in a foreign language.

"What the hell is he doing?" she whispered to the woman next to her. Mia figured the smart thing to do would be to turn and run, but her feet remained planted. Apparently, she wasn't very bright.

HADES FELT Mia's eyes on him as spectators began to line the sidewalks and watch the event unfold. So much for being anonymous, but then again, the only one who knew who he was was Mia, and he doubted she was going to tell.

He began his chant. "Children of the dark, I command you to

return home." A black hole snapped open, spinning into a vortex that reached several feet into the sky. A tornado spawned from Hell. Screams from protesting demons nearby permeated the air as their bodies were dragged—involuntarily—toward the darkness. Unfortunately, if there were any of his good demons in the area, they too would be pulled home. His spell did not differentiate between good or evil, and he had warned those close to him to leave this realm while Hades *cleaned house.*

Humans backed away, terror plastered on their faces, yet they were compelled by curiosity to watch the spectacle. As long as they kept their distance from those forced into the vortex, they would remain unharmed.

After several minutes, the funnel snapped shut indicating the cleansing was complete. Similar black holes had appeared all around the world, thus wrenching any demon from its hiding place. He closed his eyes and did a quick mental scan. Yes, all the evil had been captured and was tucked away in Hell. He set a timer which would reverse the vortex and spit everyone back out to where they originally came from at midnight tomorrow. Now, all that was left was Lowan and he felt the demigod brush his mind. The little twerp should be arriving any moment.

"You bastard!"

"Ah, right on cue." Hades turned to face his grandson and felt the color drain from his face. Lowan stood behind Mia with a blade touching her delicate throat.

"Did you really think you could break the rules and get away with it?" Lowan pushed his nose into Mia's hair and inhaled. "She stinks of you."

Hades' temper reached critical, and lightning split open the sky. Had no one learned it wasn't wise to piss him off? With several deep breaths, he managed to dial back his rage a notch, or maybe a half. He widened his stance and crossed his arms. "You're a fucking idiot and a disgrace to my DNA. I have not broken any rules, because if I had, you would be incinerated. I merely made a deal to stop your tirade and give people a reprieve." He narrowed his gaze and allowed the red in his eyes to come forth.

"Until midnight tomorrow, there will be peace. Either live with it or I will show you what real suffering is all about."

Lowan's cackle filled the air. "You seem to be missing my *point*." He pressed his blade harder against Mia's throat until tears streamed down her cheeks. "In case you hadn't noticed, I'm holding a knife against the throat of the female you marked as your own."

Hades quickly tired of this game. He had more important things to do with his limited time in the Upperworld. Like fucking for starters and the female he'd intended to do that with was in Lowan's grip. He flicked his gaze to the blade pressed against her perfect skin and watched in delight as it turned to dust and floated away. Next, he put an invisible hold around Lowan's windpipe and squeezed until the demigod dropped to his knees, releasing Mia as he went.

Hades stormed closer and was pleased to see Mia step away from Lowan. He forced his anger to recede, and hopefully his eyes returned to their normal color. "I would kill you now if given the chance and be damned the consequences. However, I relish the thought of torturing your soul for eternity once it's ripped from your body." He gave Lowan an invisible kick in the gut.

"You are a minor god, and while you may be far stronger than these humans, compared to me you are a speck on my boot. I will confine you until my agreement is up." He snapped his fingers and sent Lowan to his worst dungeon to wait out the holiday. Hades turned his attention to a trembling Mia. The desire to pull her into his arms and soothe her fears was overwhelming. Instead, he refrained from the rather new and frightening emotions bombarding him.

"T-that is your grandson?"

He held his hands up. "As much as I hate to admit it, yes."

"Then why don't you destroy him and stop all of this?" She looked around, her eyes wild. "Apparently you're powerful enough."

"Rules. And while I thoroughly enjoy breaking them, there are some even I will obey. Now, your place, or shall I find us a nice hotel?" He reverted back to his womanizing ways, hopeful she might say yes.

Her perfect pink mouth fell open before she glared at him and slammed it shut. "When Hell freezes over." Then she turned and ran.

"Well, that was rather ungrateful, and I could freeze Hell if that was your desire." He shouted after her, trying to hide his disappointment. "Very well. I have other things to take care of. For now," he muttered knowing full well he would search her out later.

CHAPTER FOUR

MIA HAD no idea where she was running to, she had panicked and bolted. A part of her was pissed as hell. How dare he assume she would simply fall into his bed. Never would she admit the desire that had ripped through her when Hades extended his invitation. It scared her senseless.

When some of her common sense came back, she headed into the store and locked the door. Her heart raced as she leaned against the glass fighting to calm herself. As her breathing settled into normal, she suddenly realized what an idiot she was.

"Mia, you dumb shit. Hades can vanish at will, he can most certainly get through a locked door." She sucked in a deep breath and turned to unlock it. No reason to keep customers away. Besides, she was now curious to learn more about what was going on. The TV blared again and caught her attention. She walked closer to hear what the newscasters were saying. Huge smiles covered their faces as they laughed and recapped the top story of how, out of nowhere, black funnels opened and sucked the demons in.

"The angel Aidyn said it would happen and it did. Merry Christmas everyone," the news anchor said.

Tears welled up behind her eyes. Painful memories swelled inside her until she thought she might literally burst. Instead, she folded them up and tucked them away and tried to fill the empty space with happier times. Memories of her younger brother Danny before drugs had taken his life on Christmas Eve. Joyful times when they were kids and helped their mother decorate the sugar cookies then sit in front of the television to watch holiday movies while sampling their tasty treats.

Her brother had only been eighteen when death wrapped its dark cloak around him and snuffed out his light. Mia had done everything to protect him, but it hadn't been enough. She was never enough for any of them to stick around.

A customer entering pulled her from the emotional abyss she was about to drown in. Looking up, she was slightly disappointed to find a woman and two small children walk into the store. What had she expected? Did she think Hades was going to waltz in and stake his claim? Her palm tingled, and she rubbed her thumb across it, but the sensation didn't abate. Instead, she offered a smile when the woman set a case of water on the counter.

"Can you believe the demons are gone?" the woman asked, swiping her card in the reader.

"I know. At least now everyone can enjoy the holiday in peace." Mia would be going home to her small apartment after her shift. Alone. Her father left when she and her brother were small and the bastard never looked back. Six months after Mia's brother Danny overdosed, her mom committed suicide. Mia's life was one big upside-down rollercoaster and she wanted off.

"Merry Christmas," the woman said.

Mia faked another smile. "Merry Christmas." Even if she was alone for the holidays, she would do like she did every year and volunteer at the local shelter. At least feeding those less fortunate reminded her how much she did have. It also gave her a sense of accomplishment and worth. Something she desperately needed as most days she fought not to sink into her pit of misery.

HADES WASN'T certain where he wanted to start. There was so much to do and so many females to spread himself around with. He wandered Bourbon Street and soaked up the intoxicating evil. Sure, his demons were tucked back into their realm, but humans had their own dark side. One bred of too much drink and a lot of sex and it was right up his alley.

He slid closer to the lovely creature wearing nothing more than glitter on her body and floss up her ass.

"Come inside for a good time," she cooed.

With a smile, he slipped his arm around her waist then wondered why he wanted to suddenly push her away. "What is this concoction you wear on your body?"

Her own smile widened. "You like? It's body paint and the rest of the girls inside are wearing it too."

The fangs tucked up in his mouth ached to free themselves. "This… I must witness for myself." Damn, he really had been locked away for far too long.

She entwined her arm around his bicep. "My name is Brandy, let me be your personal escort." Then led him through the doorway and into the dark interior. Hades being a god meant his vision was perfect in any lighting condition. Therefore, he adjusted quickly and scanned the room, noting every individual in the place. Their deepest wants and desires now at his beck and call. The place was full of so much sin his power tripled, and he had to fight the urge to unleash it right here in the middle of the room. Instead, he forced his focus back to the delicious female next to him.

"Brandy, do you taste as divine as the liquor?"

She merely giggled and continued to lead him across the room. The wooden floor beneath his boots groaning as he crossed it. His escort led him to a table in the corner where she pulled out a chair and indicated for him to sit. He settled in while she stopped another female, who also sported painted on clothing and carried a tray full of colorful liquid-filled glasses. Brandy spoke something to the other female who looked him over, a smile curving her painted mouth. Brandy snatched a tall glass containing his favorite color red and walked back to the table.

"We call this a hurricane. It's a New Orleans favorite." She set it in front of him and crawled into his lap.

Delightful. She had planted her bare ass right over his crotch. This was proving to be a grand start to his afternoon, regardless of the fact his thoughts kept creeping back to Mia. He took a sip of his drink and found it to his liking.

"This is acceptable."

Seconds later, the female who had been carrying the tray slid into the chair next to him and leaned so close her painted breasts grazed his arm.

"You're the guy on TV earlier this morning."

He grunted with disdain. Getting on the local news hadn't been in his plans but what-the-fuck-ever. He was here now, and his intentions were to enjoy every second of his freedom. Hell, at this rate he might even consider staying. It would certainly piss off Zarek and that would please Hades immensely.

"Appears I would be," he replied.

"So, what's your name, handsome?" Brandy asked.

"I am Hades, god of the Underworld."

The girls giggled.

"Well, Hades, we have a room upstairs if you'd like to join us." The other female stroked his thigh.

"Lead the way, ladies, and let me show you the best orgasm you've ever had."

Both females jumped up and as Hades grabbed his drink to follow them, his senses went on alert and he swung his focus across the room.

With a scowl, he said. "Don't start without me. I'll only be a moment." He stormed across the room to meet his brother, Argathos. "Why are you here?"

"You don't want those women, brother," Argathos said.

"Like hell I don't. Them and any other female who is willing." He wasn't one to stoop to force. Besides, his god aura was enough to make women fall in line for a chance to spend time with him. Well, except for Mia. She seemed to be a mystery, but he had more important things to do at the moment than to solve her.

"Zarek has decided since you're here, it is time."

Hades lifted a brow. "Is he certain?"

"Yes."

MIA'S SHIFT ended without any more oddities. Thank goodness because she couldn't take a whole lot more. Her walk home was much different than usual, more people milled the streets and Christmas music played from speakers mounted on the streetlights. It was hard to believe that monsters had been terrorizing humanity only hours earlier. Mia knew she should be grateful for the fact she was alive but being alone painted her world black. She often wondered how she managed to continue getting out of bed each day. Yet, she did because she was the only one to carry the memories. If she left this world then her family would be lost forever. Her mother and brother lived in her heart, and she would remember every single thing about them. Would one day pass those memories to her children, but first she had to find a way to rid herself of this damn curse.

She stopped in her tracks, lifted her hand, and once again stared at the empty space on her palm where Hades had touched her. While there was nothing to see, her skin tingled, and a sudden thought came to her. If he was a god, would he be able to help her?

"Stupid, Mia. Why did you run?" *Because he wanted to have sex with you!* And while he was all kinds of delicious, he was a freaking god. Not any god, but the lord of demons and all things bad. She chewed her lip, all kinds of crazy ideas racing through her mind. She swallowed down fear until it landed in the pit of her stomach and her decision was made. She would do anything to get her life back, and if it meant bargaining with the devil—er, Hades then that was exactly what she intended to do. First step would be to locate him. She brought herself back to the present and looked around, her gaze landing on a sign across the street.

Mirror Image.

"Perfect." She checked traffic before bolting and made a brisk walk to the other side. Once there, she stood outside with her hand on the door, hesitant to enter. She had avoided these places ever since her ex-boyfriend's mistress had placed the curse on her. Taking in a deep breath, Mia pushed the door and walked inside.

The air, thick with the scent of frankincense, slowed her racing heart.

"Hello, my name is Faye, how may I help you?" A cheery voice came from in front of her. Mia looked up from the plank floor and into the deep blue eyes of the woman smiling at her.

"Umm..."

Faye tilted her head, flipping her thick, black hair over her shoulder. "You carry a curse."

"How do you know?"

Creases appeared between the woman's brows. "I can see your aura and there is a small black stain indicating a powerful witch cursed you."

She nodded. "Yes."

"You should know that only the witch who cast it, or a member of her family, can lift it."

"Yes. I learned this right after it happened, but that's not what I'm here for." Mia shifted her weight.

"Well then, what can I do for you?"

Before she could think further and chicken out, Mia shoved her hand out, palm facing up. "Do you see anything here?"

The woman stepped closer, her gaze narrowed before it widened, and she stepped back. "Oh my. You carry Hades' marking."

Shit, so there really was something there. "He came into the store where I work and bought Twizzlers."

Faye frowned. "Twizzlers? Not exactly what I would expect." She touched Mia on the arm. "Come with me and tell me everything." She led Mia through a beaded curtain and into a back room where she offered tea and a plastic chair at a small, round table.

Once Mia was settled with her mug, Faye sat across from her. "Start from the beginning. How did you end up marked as one of Hades' females?"

Is that what the brand was? Mia hated she couldn't see it. "As I said, he came into my store and I helped him. When he asked me to hold out my hand and touched me, I had no idea why or who he was. Not until afterward when he said he was Hades and he would be back for me."

Faye shifted in her seat. "He hasn't come for you yet?"

Mia sipped her herbal tea and allowed it to warm her from the inside out. "After he cleared out the demons, that Lowan came after me and put a knife to my throat." She shivered at the memory. "Hades turned the blade to ash and sent Lowan away. It was then he asked if I wanted to get a room, but I ran."

Faye sat silent for a moment before she responded. "Interesting. You do realize if you expect me to remove the marking, I'm afraid I can't." She offered a look of sympathy.

"I figured as much, but I was thinking since Hades is a god, he might be able to lift my curse."

"I see. Well he is very powerful, and if anyone could, I would think he would be able. Are you thinking of bargaining with him?"

Mia breathed deep and slowly released it. "I am. Trouble is, I don't know how to find him."

Faye lifted her mug. "Well, sweetheart, that's the easy part. You are marked, simply call him to you."

Well, hell's bells.

HADES STARED at his brother before uttering a word. "His timing fucking sucks." He glanced over his shoulder at the painted ladies waiting for him. *Damn it!* Well, he did have a duty to perform, and then he could play while the world took a nosedive.

"Fine. I will set events into motion." He placed his glass on a nearby table then strode for the door. Once outside, he inhaled the sweet scent of sex and sin. He rather liked Bourbon Street; it was home away from home. Little did the human race realize that for every selfish deed they carried out, it only served to fuel his power. The energy crackled around him, pulsed through his veins then suddenly everything went silent.

"What the fu—" Darkness swallowed him, and he was swept through a vortex. When everything cleared, the sight that met him caused him to grin.

"Well, well. For one who recently ran from me, you quickly learned how to summon me." He advanced, and Mia's arm shot up, her hand planted on his chest to stop him from moving closer.

He laughed. "That won't stop me, but I'm willing to play whatever game you desire." He relaxed, enjoying the heat of her palm on his muscles.

"I want to make a deal."

He quirked a brow. "Interesting."

"But first, I want answers." She finally brought her arm back to her side, and he found he missed her touch.

"Fine," he sighed. It didn't matter if his deed was carried out today or next week. Events would still happen that would lead to Lowan's destruction. Hades wasn't willing to sacrifice his own pleasure with this exquisite creature in front of him. Mia shifted, her nervousness apparent and Hades had need to make her comfortable, so he moved to the sofa and took a seat.

"This your apartment, I assume?" He glanced around the small room. The furnishings were modest. Only the threadbare sofa he sat on, a coffee table, and a rickety, wooden rocking chair she had plopped in across from him. He found her lifestyle distasteful.

"Where else would I summon you to? Ritz Carlton?"

He lifted a shoulder. "I could take us to an extravagant penthouse."

"I don't need luxury."

"Obviously," he snorted.

"You're a self-centered ass," she stated without so much as a bat of her thick eyelashes.

"I am a god, what did you expect?"

"Yes, I suppose the universe revolves around you and your enormous ego." Her gaze narrowed on him. "Let me tell you something, not everyone can be surrounded by nice things, have plenty of food to eat, or even a shelter from the elements. Try living like *that* for a change."

Well, the girl had spunk. He liked it. Hades wasn't used to anyone challenging him. To do so might bring his wrath, but this... This was a breath of fresh air and he liked the mental stimulation. He leaned forward. "You wish me to live like those I see on the street?"

She let out a short laugh. "I doubt you'd last five minutes before you would be calling on your powers."

He worked his jaw. For some reason her words cut him, and he despised the feeling it evoked. "You have no idea what it's like to be stuck in a realm with nothing but evil surrounding you. You cannot leave unless summoned. It is..." He took in a breath. "It is its own prison."

Her eyes widened. Had his statement caught her off guard?

"You didn't think a god could suffer, did you?" He wasn't even sure why he had made the statement.

She relaxed into her rocker. "No. I guess everyone has their cross to bear."

"Surely you didn't summon me to ridicule my lifestyle."

"No." She straightened. "Why did you mark me?"

Now there was an excellent question. "I was asked to come here to rescue your holiday. Upon entering your realm, you were the first female I came across. I marked you, so I could find you later."

She licked her lips. "You only wanted to fuck me." Disappointment sounded in her voice.

"And I still do."

The flecks of silver swirling in her eyes spoke volumes of her anger. "There are plenty of women who would willingly have sex with you."

"You are not one of them?"

"My body is not for sale," she spat.

"Pity. Most would be honored to be chosen."

CHAPTER FIVE

FURY SETTLED into Mia's blood. Just who the hell did he think he was? Oh, right. The god of the Underworld, well la-de-fucking-da!

"You! You, egotistical bastard! What makes you think all women will drop at your feet and become subservient?"

He grinned. "Because they always do."

She balled her fists. "Gah!" She wanted to punch the smirk off his handsome face.

He straight out laughed. Laughed until she swore tears were going to roll down his cheeks and her anger grew. Why had she thought to invite him here? Oh wait, she wanted his help. Now the thought of asking him for anything sank like a shipwreck at sea. She did have her pride if nothing else.

"I cannot remember when I had so much fun. There are few who ever dare to be themselves with me. I like you, Mia. You are a breath of fresh air."

She slowed her breathing and tried to regain control of her emotions. Words he had uttered earlier about his home being its own prison came back to her. Could a god actually suffer? It might explain why he was the way he was. Certainly, the demons bowed to him. Did he expect her to do the same?

"Mia?"

That silky, sinful voice pulled her from her thoughts, and she stared into his deep brown eyes. For the first time she saw a spark of pain hidden in their depths. What had this man before her seen in his lifetime?

"What did you call me here for?" His tone now gentle.

"I thought since you were a god, you might be able to break my curse."

His gaze narrowed on her and bore into her until she felt completely naked beneath his stare. Moments ticked by before he finally spoke again.

"I hadn't seen it before, but it is there buried deep. Who did this to you?"

"An ex's girlfriend." Suddenly she didn't want to reveal the story. Had no desire to bare her soul and the pain that still resided there.

He leaned back into his seat. "Tell me." It was a command and she wondered if she shouldn't simply tell him to leave. This was a bad idea.

She looked away from him and suddenly felt tiny in his presence. "I caught my boyfriend cheating, and when I confronted them, that was when she placed the curse on me."

"The woman is a powerful witch," he commented.

"I guess." She shrugged, her inadequacy never more evident. Her family hadn't loved her enough to stick around and neither had her boyfriend. Mia often wondered if she might ever find happiness. Would ever have a man who was devoted to her and the family she craved. Perhaps she was meant to forever be alone.

He leaned forward again, his lids hooded. There was no way to stop the shudder that crept up her spine. Desire swirled in his eyes like a storm ready to unleash its fury on the world. No man had ever looked at her like this. She swallowed. "I..." She had no idea what to say.

"As far as your family? Your brother couldn't deal with your father abandoning him. Your mother lost her faith, but they loved you. Even your father did, which is why he left. The boyfriend however, he was a complete idiot and not deserving of a woman such as yourself."

Her lungs seized as she flicked her gaze back up to him. "How—?"

He held his hand up. "I am a god. I see everything."

"But if you knew then why ask me what happened?" Her anger grew again. Was he playing with her?

"I didn't know until I looked into your soul and saw it for myself. Saw your pain, your desires."

Mia might as well be naked for Hades had stripped her bare. Had seen things about her she never wanted any human to see. Vulnerable didn't even begin to describe how she felt right now. Crawling out of the room actually crossed her mind. Instead, she shifted in her seat under his heated stare. "Can you remove the curse or not?" No sense in beating around the bush.

"I can, but it comes with a price."

"I'm not giving you my soul." She wasn't even sure she still had one, but if she did, she would not be offering it to the devil.

He scowled. "I told you, I am Hades!"

"You can—"

"Hear your thoughts? Clearly."

She dug her nails into her palms until the pain was almost unbearable. "That's wrong."

"Perhaps, but I don't do it intentionally."

She jumped from her rocker, unable to take his eyes boring into her any longer. It was unsettling.

"I don't want your soul, Mia. And yes, you still have one."

She paced her tiny apartment. "I'm not sleeping with you either." This time she whirled and stared him down. Pulling on her inner strength, she tried not to notice how sexy he was. How seductive his smile, or the way the light played across his darkened jaw. No, she refused to notice the desire sparking in his eyes. Would never admit that his desire sparked something deep inside her. Something that wanted to welcome her naughty side. Even encourage it to come out and play.

"While that does disappoint me greatly, that is not what I require from you."

"What then?" What else did she have to offer?

"You will come reside in my home for thirty days."

She stepped back. "If I am not to sleep with you then what? Become your servant?"

He rose, and his height had her stepping back farther. "No. You will be a guest and treated as such."

Now she was totally confused. "Why would you want me to stay with you?"

"Only for the company."

"Oh." How lonely was he?

"What about my job? I can't simply leave for a month." Seriously, did he not think of these things?

He waved her off. "Time between our realms is different. You won't even be missed."

No. She supposed there was no one left to miss her. "Really?"

"Yes. You will only be gone hours according to your world," he assured.

"Okay then." If she had to be Hades' guest in order to release her from this curse, then so be it. It would be a small price to pay.

HADES HAD INDEED INTENDED to ask Mia for more in order to remove her curse. It was his nature to make such demands of sex, blood, and one's soul. However, when it came time to name his price, he found while he desired Mia as a woman, he wanted her to desire him as well. She did. This he knew with certainty, but he wanted her to come to him of her own free will.

Holy hell. Was he going soft? He had no idea what came over him, but he had named his terms therefore he would not change them. Hades was nothing if not a man of his word.

"How can I trust you?" she asked.

"A contract will be drawn and signed by both of us, and blood will bind it." Her eyes widened at the word *blood* and he held up his hand. "Only a drop on the contract from each of us, though I will admit to wondering what you taste like, Mia."

She swallowed. "I will get to review this contract before I'm expected to sign?"

"Yes. I will have it drawn up and dropped off by courier. Now, I have duties to attend to, but you know how to reach me should you have questions." He faded away, keeping her in his sight until he was carried away by his power. Next stop was to pay a visit to a certain dragon shifter. Moments later, he located said shifter perched high up in the Carpathian Mountains. She immediately sensed his presence and jumped to her feet then tilted her head when her deep blue gazed landed on him.

"Hades." She offered a slight bow. "I heard rumor you were in our realm."

"It's freezing up here." Snow whipped around his legs and he decided he had no use for the white, fluffy stuff. Much preferring the tropical clime.

She stared into the distance, something was definitely bothering her. "I come here when I need to think."

He scoffed. "I'm not sure how one could think of anything with their balls freezing. Course, you wouldn't have that problem."

She laughed. Something he understood she did little of. "I suppose it is quite the difference from what you're used to."

"We need to talk, Leria. Perhaps we can move to a more suitable location?" He held out his hand. She hesitated only briefly before slipping her hand into his. When he curled his fingers around hers, he flashed them to his favorite place. Waves crashed on the shore and Hades sighed. "This is much more preferable."

"Why do you seek me out?" she asked as he started to walk.

"Leria, my dear, I will get straight to the point. You are already aware your chosen mate is the vampire king, Aidyn?"

"Yes." Disgust punctuated her reply.

"He committed the most grievous crime against the gods and must pay the price."

"I thought he had already paid his price. I saw the scars on his body, and he told me they were from his punishment."

"Yes, but he has yet to pay me." Hades stopped and faced her. Time to make his request.

"What does any of this have to do with me?"

"You will do my bidding, Leria. You will make sure the vampire serves his sentence."

A frown creased her forehead. "What is his punishment?"

"Death."

She stepped back, her face drawn into panic. "True death of an immortal?" she whispered.

"Yes. I will procure the dagger of Embara for you and you will shove it into his heart. Once the deed is completed, you will return the blade to me as it must remain in hiding until my brother the Phoenix god rises again."

"What did he do that would bring his death?"

"That is only for the gods to know."

She shook her head. "I cannot do this. I don't even understand why you would ask this of me."

"Yet not long ago you threatened him yourself. He took away the one thing you loved most. Your father. Even refused to allow you to say goodbye to the man before he took your father's life." When Leria had been a child, her father Odage had been corrupted by Lowan and had killed the queen, the vampire king's mother. When the dragon shifter had finally been captured, the king sentenced the dragon to death for his crimes.

Anger and pain flashed in the female's eyes. "This is true, but why don't you simply take him yourself?"

Hades stared into Leria's soul. Conflict resided there. Yes, she wanted revenge for her father, who had been under the influence of a powerful demigod. But the girl also felt the pull of her mate.

"You are what he desires most in this world. What more fitting end than seeing you terminate his life?" He narrowed his gaze. "It will be your only chance to avenge your father. If Aidyn dies by another hand, you will lose that chance forever."

"Why? Why did the gods decide to make Aidyn my mate?" Her bottom lip trembled.

Hades shrugged. "It was Zarek's call. Who knows what goes through my brother's twisted mind."

"If I refuse?"

Hades waved his arm and forced Leria to view the scene in front of her. "Watch what the king did to your father." Her eyes grew wider as she witnessed her father, chained and begging to be spared as the vampire king himself wielded the sword that sliced the shifter's head off.

"Stop!" Leria cried, the tears finally spilling down her cheeks.

Hades shut down the image and straightened to his full height. "You are commanded to do the will of the gods, Leria. Kill your mate."

This time fire flashed in her eyes, the deep blue shifting to the green of the dragon. "Bring me the dagger and I will do your bidding."

"It will be done." Hades grinned.

WHEN THE DOORBELL RANG, Mia froze in her spot. She

wasn't expecting company so figured it must be the courier. She managed to unstick herself from her seat and answer the door. An attractive, young man stood on the other side with a large envelope in his hand.

"Ms. Brown?"

"Y-yes."

He inclined his head. "I have a packet for you. When you have looked it over and signed the documents, they will arrive to the owner on their own."

"I don't understand," she said accepting the large, brown envelope.

"Simply, once you sign, the documents will vanish and arrive on Hades' desk."

"Oh." Well, how convenient. "Thank you. Is there anything else?"

"No, ma'am. Enjoy your holiday." He vanished into thin air, causing Mia to jump. You'd think she would be used to it by now. After closing the door, she dropped the envelope on the counter, her shoulders slumping forward. She had forgotten it was Christmas Eve and hated the reminder. Wandering to the sliding door, she pulled aside the curtain and stared into the darkness. Her gaze followed the colorful lights that danced along the street. Opening the door, she stepped onto the small balcony where carolers' songs filled the night air. Before she realized, she was caught up in the music, humming along to familiar songs from her childhood. Her heart filled with sadness and loneliness sank deep, chilling her to the bone. She turned and went back inside, closing the door behind her and leaving all the holiday cheer on the other side. Through unshed tears, she stared at the envelope. It almost appeared to glow, and she thought for a moment she had lost her mind. Of course it would glow, with Hades anything was possible.

Taking a breath to calm herself, she reached for the envelope and noticed a wax seal. Bringing it closer, she ran her fingers over the serpent that adorned the red wax. Before she could change her mind, she opened it and pulled out the papers. At first glance they appeared like any contract, but she understood who she was dealing with and didn't trust him. For a moment she wondered if legal counsel would be wise, but then what would she say?

"Oh hey, can you look at my contract with the devil? Oops, I mean Hades?"

She'd be laughed right out of the office. Even with the current events, many people were still in denial of demons and angels. With a sigh, she brought her attention back to the papers in her hand, curled up on the couch, and began to read. An hour later she had gone over every detail twice. From everything she read, the list of requirements appeared reasonable. She glanced at them again.

- Reside in Hades' palace in Hell for thirty (30) days.
- Dine with Hades at his table every evening.
- Wear clothing and jewelry selected by Hades while in his presence.
- May not venture outside the palace gates without an escort approved by Hades.

THAT THIRD ONE concerned her a bit. She chewed her lip, grabbed a pen, and added her demands.

- Wear clothing and jewelry selected by the Hades while in his presence. **(Clothing will fully cover breasts, buttocks, and genitalia.)** *MB*

IN RETURN, he promised the following:

- A private suite.
- All clothing and jewelry provided may be kept at the end of this contract.
- Full protection while in Hades' palace as well as outside the gates.
- Hades, or anyone else residing in Hell, will not make demands for sexual favors. Any such activity will be at the discretion of Mia Brown only.
- At the termination of this contract, Hades will remove the curse placed on Mia Brown.

THE REST SEEMED good enough and she didn't see any hidden meanings, so she signed where indicated. As soon as that was done, a small circle appeared on the paper next to her signature. Instructions indicated this was where her drop of blood was supposed to go. A finger pricker rolled out of the envelope and stopped in front of her.

"Well, what do you know." She shook her head, picked up the instrument, and jabbed her middle finger, allowing a drop of blood to hit the paper. The second her body fluid saturated the parchment, the contract vanished from the coffee table.

"Damn, he wasn't kidding." Seconds later, the papers arrived back on the table with a note attached.

DEAREST MIA,

I WAS sorry to see you wish to remain so modest, but I agree to your terms. I have signed and returned your copy. Be ready to leave at midnight on Christmas Day. You will not require luggage as everything will be provided for you.

. . .

SINCERELY,

Hades

SHE SIGHED, unable to believe she had just agreed to reside in Hell for thirty days.

CHAPTER SIX

HADES HAD CONVINCED Leria to kill the vampire king, so now he had to procure the dagger. He opened his mind and sent the mental command for the new goddess, Katie, to come to him at once. Moments later, a bitching redhead landed on the beach in front of him.

"What the fucking hell?" she hissed. The female had a mouth any sailor would be proud of and she pinned him with a fiery glare. "How did you do that?"

"I outrank you."

She shoved her fists on her hips, her rather pregnant belly protruding. "Well, that just sucks donkey balls." Her brow quirked. "So, can I do that to someone else? Command them to appear and drag their sorry-ass out of say...the shower?"

He chuckled. "You are a wicked woman. Only if you outrank them and currently, I'm not aware of any newly established gods or goddesses."

"Bummer. So, while the beach is a lovely view, my mate is likely freaking out right now since I simply vanished. Besides, it's Christmas. Why am I here?"

"I need the dagger of Embara."

Her gaze narrowed again. "Why?"

"I am your superior, therefore not required to answer to you." His patience waned. He was ready for this day to be done, so tomorrow at midnight he could collect his new houseguest. For whatever reason, he was actually excited about something for once in a long time.

"I'm not handing the dagger over for no good reason." Her power flared; she intended to flee but he held her there with his own flash of power.

"Let me go, asshole!"

He folded his arms over his chest. "That the best you got?"

"I can dish out a lot more if you'd like."

"While I'd love to stand here and spar with you, I have a job to do, which is to start waking your father. Now, give me the damn blade or I will rip your home to shreds to find it." She needn't know the truth behind why he desired the dagger.

Her eyes widened. "You wouldn't dare!"

He closed the space between them. "Fucking try me. I'm Hades and destruction runs through my veins. You won't even have a splinter of wood left to identify when I'm done."

"You would do that to your own family? Uncle?" She batted her lashes as if that would help her cause.

"You should know, *niece*. You carry the blood of my father as well as I do. What would you do?"

"No need to get testy." She rubbed her belly. "Fine, but only because I'm anxious for my father to waken and not because you're a bully." She held out her hand and the dagger flashed into her palm.

He reached for it. "I understand your concerns, and I promise, once my brother is fully awake the dagger will be returned to him."

She gave a nod and released the blade. "We need him to end this nightmare." She glanced down at her rather large stomach. "I want my child to have at least one grandparent."

"Well, technically since Zarek is Seth's creator, that would make him the child's grandfather."

Katie wrinkled her nose.

"Zarek lost his only daughter long ago." She had sacrificed herself to create the guardians. "And your father, Pyros, will be pleased to have a babe in the family. We all would."

She gave a nod. "I'd better get home."

Hades stepped back and tipped his head. "Enjoy your holiday, niece." He released his power over her and she flashed away. Once alone, he studied the dagger. It was simple in design, considering what it was intended for. The blade was six inches of cold steel he had forged himself for his brother. The handle, well-worn bone carved from the thigh of a demon. The small symbols—one for each brother—etched into the handle were the final piece of the puzzle that completed the immortal killer. The dagger vibrated with the power of the gods, and even Hades had to swallow bile at the thought of the destructive instrument he and his brothers had created.

Securing the blade into a sheath strapped to his chest, he flashed from the area and headed straight for the Draki's old home in Vandeldor. The shifters had gone back to the mountains after Lowan and his minions vacated, and the dragons were now busy trying to rebuild. Hades located Leria near a large bonfire.

He cloaked himself and approached the young girl. "Leria."

To her credit she gave nothing away, simply slipped away from the fire and into the darkness where he followed. Once far enough from the others, she stopped and turned.

"I have the dagger." He opened his coat to reveal the blade strapped to his chest. Her gaze darted to the dagger.

"It is plain looking. I imagined something more ornate."

"It was made to kill not admire."

Her gaze flicked back up to his and she swallowed. "Of course."

"Are you having second thoughts?" He sensed the turmoil inside her. "The king killed your father and you despise him for it."

Her eyes blazed with anger. "I vowed to him that he would die from my hand. I intend to keep that promise."

"Good." He pulled the blade from the sheath and offered it to her. "I will collect this when you are finished."

She eyed him with suspicion. "How do you know it won't be used against you?"

"Because all of the gods will be watching your every move. You wouldn't get far in that endeavor."

"Just checking." She smiled, and Hades admired her backbone. He experienced actual guilt for the turmoil he was about to put her through. She might hold her mate—the vampire king—in ill regard at the moment, but when she took his life her heart would shatter.

"Stay to your path, Leria. I am counting on you." He vanished before she responded and took himself to the street outside Mia's apartment.

MIA TRIED TO SLEEP, but as usual it was a worthless feat. Once again, at the stroke of 11:00 pm she found herself slipping through her mattress and onto the floor below. Her body shifting—like it did every night since the curse—into a spirit. She stared up at the underside of her bed.

"Damn it!" You'd think she would learn to simply get out of bed before the shifting occurred. It was rather disturbing to pass through a mattress. With a sigh she managed to slip out and get situated. Well, as much as one could when turned into a ghost. It had taken her almost a year after the curse to figure out how to leave her apartment. Once she had, she discovered a much darker side to her world. Wandering the streets, Mia found she was able to see people's emotions. First it started out as colors, but then she began to feel them herself. Take them on as her own. There was so much desperation in her community and it tore her apart. She tried to reach those who needed help the most, but she wasn't able to communicate. If only she could reach their minds and ease their suffering. She quickly realized what Hades must see when he looked at someone.

Floating across the floor, she went to the window and stared out. The streets were quiet, likely everyone tucked in bed and waiting for Christmas morning. She couldn't wait for morning, or to be exact 4:00 am, when she would become corporeal again. Until such time, she floated about her apartment and watched the clock tick. Every night, five hours of her life were taken away. As she moved past a mirror, she stopped and stared at herself. Translucent, she had already learned not many saw her if she ventured out. It took an extreme amount of energy to become visible and not worth how she felt afterwards. There wasn't a hangover in the world that compared. Mia also worried one day she would be stuck like this and simply fade away. Would anyone even miss her? Doubtful since she had no family left and her employer would simply replace her.

She moved on, mindlessly milling about until finally her body returned to normal. Exhausted as usual, she went and slipped on a pair of cozy socks and padded across the bedroom floor, making her way to the Keurig, one of the few luxuries she allowed herself.

Shoving a pod into the machine, she patiently waited while the room filled with the aroma of coffee. Adding a splash of skim milk and a dribble of caramel syrup, she headed for the couch. Might as well see what was on the TV. No sooner had she started flipping through way too many channels of Christmas music, prayers, and utter nonsense, she realized she was no longer alone in the room.

Her muscles tensed until they ached, and she slowly turned her head to glance at the man standing to her right. Relief quickly followed by panic slid over her skin. "It's not time yet."

"Don't worry, my dear Mia. I'm not here to collect you yet." He held out a large beautifully wrapped package. "A gift for you to start your day."

"A gift?" She never moved from her seat.

"Yes, Mia, you do know what a gift is." He moved closer and it was hard for her to miss the sex appeal that rolled off him. It coated her skin and left an aching between her thighs. Suddenly the thin tank and yoga pants she wore didn't feel like enough. His gaze dropped briefly to her breasts, and she didn't need to look to know that her nipples pushed hard against the fabric. It was as if her body begged him to touch her. Fortunately, he didn't stare nor did he comment.

"Why would you bring me a gift?"

He sat next to her and she was certain the very air surrounding him reached out and caressed her. It was all she could do not to crawl into his lap, but she held her ground. This man would not know how much he ignited her desire. How really lonely she was.

"I thought you humans celebrated this day with gifts and feasting. Was I wrong?"

Her temple throbbed. "Really? You humans?"

His brow arched. "You are human, Mia."

"It's impolite to point it out." She sipped her coffee, clutching the mug a little too tight. "It makes you sound arrogant."

"But I am arrogant."

She eyed him. "There is no reason to be."

"I annoy you."

"Very much." For more reasons than she cared to admit. She took another sip of her coffee and tried to pretend he wasn't there. When he grinned, she found herself wondering if his lips were as soft as they appeared. He smiled wider, flashing perfect teeth except for the fangs, but even those evoked a sense of sexual desire. She quickly looked away, tried to slow her racing pulse, and told herself she only desired him because it had been far too long since a man had touched her.

"Mia, you should not be ashamed of your desires. They are perfectly normal."

She worked her jaw. "I have no desire and you should stop using your power to compel me."

"I am using no power against you."

She glared at him. "And don't lie to me about it. It's not nice to play games like this." She felt slightly better blaming him for her predicament.

"I am not lying. How long has it been since you lain with a man?"

Her jaw dropped. "None of your business."

"You should learn to own your feelings, Mia, otherwise they own you. Sexual desire is nothing to be ashamed of. Wanting someone is not a bad thing and I freely admit to wanting you."

She opened her mouth to speak, but he held up a hand.

"I stick to my word. I will make no advances toward you, and I vow I am not trying to compel you. I will patiently wait for you to come to me."

Thank god she'd not been drinking her coffee because she would have spit it in his face. "I don't think that's going to happen."

He lifted a shoulder. "Perhaps. But be warned, sex is everywhere in Hell. You may see some things your delicate nature might cringe at."

"I don't have a delicate nature." Oh shit, what was she going to see? She'd never thought of things that might go on right under her nose.

"Very well. My gift." He shoved the gold and red package at her. "There are no strings attached. It's a simple gift."

Hesitant yet curious, she relented and accepted the pretty box, which took up her entire lap. "Thank you." She was careful not to break the ribbon but slid it off with its curled bow intact. Next, she picked at the tape until the paper fell away to reveal a box with the words Oscar de la Renta embossed on the top. While Mia didn't run in the money circles, she knew enough to realize the box alone was probably worth more than her entire wardrobe.

Her hands shaking, she pulled the top off and pushed aside the gold paper then gasped.

"Oh my..." The rest of the words caught in her throat. On top was a smoldering red sweater so luxurious she wanted to crawl inside it. Underneath, a pair of straight leg jeans, the denim nearly as soft as the sweater. She was careful to set the clothes aside, so she could see what was wrapped in more tissue beneath. Caramel colored, calf-high boots so supple she couldn't wait to slip them on.

"Everything is so beautiful, but it's too much and I cannot accept it." She started to place the lid back on the box.

"You agreed to wear clothing chosen for you. I made sure this covered all of your...*assets*."

She studied him. "But our contract hasn't started yet." What would she owe him for this?

"It is a gift, one that makes me happy to give. I don't have many happy moments, Mia. Please do me the honor of accepting it and wearing the items today."

He doesn't have many happy moments? "All right. Thank you. This is the nicest thing anyone has ever given me." Before she could stop herself, she leaned closer and kissed him on the cheek. Lingered far too long before she drew back with her own face heated.

His grin went from ear to ear. "If gifts from me make you this happy, then I shall enjoy indulging you."

She quickly looked away, wondering what beast she had just woken inside of both of them.

HADES ENJOYED the smile on Mia's face when she opened her present. Her expression lacked what so many others held when he presented them with a gift. Entitlement. All who surrounded him felt they were entitled to his gifts, attention, and power. After all, they gave of themselves. Their loyalty—though technically it was bought—their bodies, and often their souls were offered up in exchange. Mia was different, however. Her smile genuine and the only thing she wanted in return was her curse gone so she could live a normal life. So she could finally find true love and start a family.

He'd seen her hopes, her dreams and understood them. They had once been his own. But he was the god of evil, and those things were not within his grasp. He would never trust a female to love him for who he was and not what he could offer.

"Enjoy the gift, Mia. I'll be back at our agreed time to pick you up." Before he could leave, she stopped him.

"Now that you have given humanity their holiday, how will you spend yours?"

Her question caught him off guard. "I do not celebrate such things."

She chewed her lip and jealousy sprang to life. He wanted to be the one to taste the plump flesh.

"What are you doing for the day, then?"

He hadn't thought about it, really. Likely go back to Bourbon Street since he had nowhere else to be. He would have to remain in this world until midnight when things would reverse and the demons and Lowan returned to their war. "I have no plans, except perhaps visiting with my brother." He did want to spend some time with Argathos.

"You have a brother?"

"I have two living currently."

"Well, enjoy your visit." There was a hint of sadness in her voice. It was then he really took a moment to look around. Mia had no decorations. No tree. None of the usual items those who celebrated the holiday would have.

"What are your plans?" He knew she had no family.

"I will be going to the local shelter and helping serve dinner later this morning."

Why did this not surprise him? Mia had a big heart and he clearly saw her scooping mashed potatoes onto the plate of some homeless person. An idea suddenly came to him.

"What time will you be back here?"

"I dunno. Maybe five. Why?"

"I will meet you back here for dinner and don't worry, I will take care of everything. How does that sound?" He liked how her eyes lit up.

"Seriously?"

"Yes. Consider it a highlight of what is to come."

"All right. I will see you then."

Hades used the door this time and walked down her hall. He hated the wretched roach-infested building she lived in and was looking forward to showing her his palace. He'd already ordered his servants to ready the suite across from his own. Anything other than perfection would be met with severe punishment. He'd better not find even one speck of dust in her rooms or his wrath would prove fatal.

CHAPTER SEVEN

MIA HURRIED AND SHOWERED, not lingering after spending way too much time chatting it up with Hades. Once toweled off, she slipped on the new clothes he brought her and felt like an absolute princess. Never had her skin touched anything so soft. With clothes nicer than any she owned, she decided a bit of makeup was called for. Usually she didn't wear it, but a swipe of gloss, a touch of blush, and mascara had her feeling beautiful. She pulled on the leather boots and decided she was going to skip the entire way to the shelter, her feet felt so good.

Grabbing a jacket and her keys, she headed out the door. Outside, the sounds of Christmas sang through the crisp morning air. She pulled the jacket tight around her neck to ward off the harsh breeze and headed down the sidewalk. The shelter was only four blocks from her apartment but was into the wind the entire way, making her wish she had grabbed a pair of gloves.

Inside, she shed the coat and placed it on a hook in exchange for an apron. There was no way she was taking any chances of spilling on her new clothes. Suddenly, she was filled with remorse. Hades had given her an exceptional gift, yet she had nothing to offer him.

There wasn't a store in town open today to get anything either. Besides, what did one get the god of Hell? He did say he didn't celebrate the holiday, but still...

"Morning, Mia."

"Morning, Michael." She greeted the manager of the shelter. Michael was a thirty-five-year-old who ran his own business as well as kept the shelter going. He was also a transplant from California, having lived in New Orleans for five years now. She'd had a crush on him when he'd first arrived, but with the curse, she had refused a date with him when he'd asked. Finally, he'd tired of waiting for her to change her mind and moved on. Now, Michael was engaged and would be marrying in the spring. It was difficult not to be jealous, but she was happy for him.

"We're going to be shorthanded for a while. Betty has family matters and will be in later," he said not ever bothering to give her a second look.

"I'm sure we'll manage. I hope everything's okay."

"She said not to worry."

"Good." Mia moved past Michael and into the kitchen, where those who'd been here since the crack of dawn cooking were busy filling trays. She grabbed one and headed for the dining room, depositing it over the warmer.

"We're ready to start serving," one of the helpers said.

Mia took a spot in front of the mashed potatoes and put on her best smile. She really did love helping out those who were less fortunate. It was the only thing that gave her a sense of satisfaction and put her life back into perspective. As people who had nothing left in the world filed past her full of thanks and holiday cheer, she was once again reminded that her problems were small in comparison. She scooped a spoonful of potatoes onto the plate of Mr. Benson, a gentleman of African-American descent, who she guessed was nearing seventy or so. He had once been a teacher in one of the poorer neighborhoods of New Orleans. When the last hurricane hit, he had lost everything and with no insurance, there was no money to replace his home. He'd been living at the shelter for the past two years, yet he never uttered a negative word about his plight.

"Morning, Ms. Brown. I'll be in the kitchen later to help with the dishes."

She smiled. "Morning, Mr. Benson. We'll be happy for the help."

"Please girl, how many times must I tell you to call me James?"

She gave a nod. "Only if you stop calling me Ms. Brown and call me Mia."

"We have an agreement then." He grinned and moved down the line.

Two hours and several full bellies later, someone played the piano. People gathered around and began singing while Mia and the others carried the empty trays back to the kitchen and started the cleanup. As promised, James was elbow deep in soapsuds washing dishes while he hummed along with the carolers.

"You seem far away, Mia."

She exchanged her already soaked towel for a dry one. No way was she going to admit her mind was on a sexy god who was having dinner with her later. She wondered what he was up to. "I was just thinking of my family."

He gave a nod. "I understand that. Sometimes I think they are better off not being here. With everything going on in the world today, that is."

"True. I hate to think of my family being hurt or worse by those demons." She'd seen enough of their destruction up close and personal. The thought of living in Hell for any length of time had her shivering.

"I've been thinking of going to meet with that Aidyn fellow about what I might do to help." James stared into the dishwater.

Mia set down her towel and touched his arm. "You're not thinking of becoming one of them, are you?"

He chuckled. "Oh, heavens no. I understand when the change occurs you will be frozen at your current age. I'm much too old for that, but there must be some way for me to help."

"I see." She picked up her towel and began drying. Her mind again wandered back to Hades.

HADES STRODE DOWN THE STREET, opening his mind to his brothers.

Argathos, Zarek, the girl is in possession of the dagger.

Seconds later, both brothers appeared in his path. Zarek crossed his arms and took a wide stance. Was Hades supposed to be intimidated? Not fucking likely. He was more than happy to go toe-to-toe with his elder brother. Matter of fact, he would love nothing more.

"Then we can expect it to happen today," Zarek stated.

"And why is that?" Hades asked.

"The guardians are holding a celebration in Vandeldor with the shifters. It will be the perfect setting for Leria to carry out your orders."

"Perfect. When do we expect them to gather?"

"This evening," Argathos replied then smiled. "You still have plenty of time to carry out your own plans."

Hades drew in a deep breath. "Perhaps you and I need to have a chat, brother."

"Yes. I think we do," Argathos said.

Hades had already set his minions to work on Mia's apartment. They were ordered to make it look like Christmas had retched its glittery cheer everywhere. He hoped when she returned, she would find her home transformed into a wonderland of holiday on steroids. "I have nothing but time at the moment."

"I have things to do. I will leave you both to your secrets, but I will summon you later." Zarek vanished.

"I see he's still an ass." Hades started to walk again, not sure where he was even headed. He knew that even with Christmas cheer all around, New Orleans still fueled the dark side of him. There was, however, one thing he intended to do before he returned to Mia's apartment.

"Zarek has changed, but I know you've not been here to see it." Argathos walked beside him.

"Whatever." Hades was quick to dismiss the statement. Still angry with his eldest brother for the centuries of torture Hades had lived with. Even using the rationale that Hades had been too much like his father, wild and downright mean, did little to make him feel better. Zarek was the king of gods, his word law. He had a beautiful wife as well. Something Hades would never admit he longed for. Family came with sacrifices though. Zarek's only daughter had given her life for the creation of the guardian Seth. Argathos had long ago lost the woman he loved, and war had broken out causing the death of their brother, Pyros. Seemed they all had paid a price. Except for him. He had never fallen in love and wasn't about to start any time in the next ten centuries.

"You need to find happiness, brother." Argathos tore Hades out of his pity party.

"Have you ever been to Hell? No, you haven't. It's full of misery and not exactly the ideal conditions for being joyful. I've even grown bored with torture and am actually considering staying here." There, he'd said it.

Argathos stopped. "You know you can't stay here, but there is no reason you cannot find what you're searching for. I'm even certain Zarek will consider lifting your sentence so you may move between realms without a summons. You only need ask him."

Hades broke out into a fit of laughter. "You seriously want me to ask Zarek for a favor? I think your crystal ball has cracked."

His brother crossed his arms. "You know I don't use such a thing." He leaned closer. "Your world is about to change, Hades. You will be brought to your knees by a female. Like it or not."

He laughed even harder. "Now I know you're delusional. You've not seen what I'm capable of, *brother*. The acts I've ordered be done to those who are condemned to my realm," he snarled. "I've been with more females than you have ever even met and not one has come close to bringing me to my knees. I am our father's son more than you know."

Argathos only shook his head. "You will soon learn the hard way."

Hades started walking, his pace even faster than before. He would never admit his brother had rattled him. Argathos was the god of visions and a seerer. He had been known to predict future events with exact accuracy. However, the god was not able to see his own future. Had that been the case, Hades was certain Argathos would have prevented his own wife, Brianna's death. Even Hades cringed at the memories of that day. He was surprised his brother had remained sane after that.

Argathos grabbed Hades' arm. "Just keep my words in mind." Argathos smiled. "I promise, Hades, you will find happiness." He backed away. "I will see you later." Then he was gone with the wind that swirled over the street.

Hades swallowed and for a moment, weakness had his muscles softening. He was quick to regain himself and remember who he was. He was Hades, god of all evil, and his torture was known in Hell and beyond. Humans and demons quaked at the mention of his name. Any female foolish enough to become his would quickly grow to regret it.

MIA HURRIED out of the shelter and down the street toward her apartment. For some strange reason, she was excited to see what Hades had planned. There was a time when Christmas had been her favorite holiday, and she wished she could once again find the spirit of the season. No matter how hard she tried, she hadn't been able to erase the bad memories associated with it. Her brother's death hung like a black cloud over her but was also the reason she did volunteer work. When her brother had been deep into the drugs, he had lived on the street. If she was able to bring even a little hope into someone else's life, then maybe it would spare another person the same grief she suffered.

When she approached her building, she hesitated at the entrance. Drawing on her courage, she opened the door and climbed the stairs. Once at the second story, she walked the creaky floors to the end of the hall where her apartment was and fumbled for her key. The door swung open before she was able to retrieve it and... Oh. My. God!

"You cut your hair and..." She leaned closer. "Your eyes are blue." The most intense steel blue she'd ever seen. With his much shorter hair, it brought out his strong jaw covered with the dark dusting of whiskers. And the short curl that fell across his forehead only added to the desire she had to run her fingers through the thick, black mass.

"I felt I needed a change. Do you approve?"

Did he seriously need her approval? Her gaze fell to the black, button-down shirt that was open just enough to allow a hint of what lay beneath. His ensemble was completed by dark jeans and boots. "I like the shorter hair. It suits you." She dared not say any more than that.

"The eyes...seem to change with my mood since I've been in your world. I'm not sure why though. Your new clothes suit you. Do you like them?"

"Umm. Y-yes, they are very nice," she managed to stutter while still trying not to stare. His gaze, now almost as dark as his shirt, bore right through her. Finally, he stepped back and waved her into the small foyer. When she walked through the door he didn't bother moving, and there was no possible way to get past his large frame without some kind of bodily contact. She turned and slid by, her hands instinctively went up and touched his chest. A firm, muscular chest that promised a view of manly perfection should he take off his shirt.

Mia managed to pull her thoughts from such nonsense and

continued into the room where she swore she was in the wrong apartment.

"What do you think?"

"Holy shit!"

Hades let out a deep laugh and she found even that sexy as hell. Mia rubbed her temples, wondering if she had hit her head on the way home. No normal thinking female would find the laugh of the god of the Underworld sexy.

"I've never seen the like... Hell, my apartment has never seen the likes of so much holiday." The biggest tree she had ever had was stuffed into the corner and decked out with lights, old-fashioned glass balls, and tinsel. It shimmered like something from an overdone Christmas card. Several poinsettias of varying sizes were placed on the floor, table, and shelves. She glanced toward the ceiling and her jaw went slack.

"Please tell me I'm not standing under mistletoe?" She looked at Hades whose grin spoke of seduction.

"You most certainly are. You can't have Christmas without it."

She quickly stepped back, her heart racing. "That's not playing fair."

He laughed. "I am Hades and I never play fair. If I did, those under me would try and take advantage." He moved closer. "You owe me a kiss, Mia."

"No, you promised." She took another step back.

"I promised not to have sex with you and a kiss is a far cry from fucking you." He didn't move closer, but his presence slid across her skin and she was forced to hide a shiver.

"Still not fair."

"Are you afraid of yourself?" One side of his mouth curled upward.

"That makes no sense. I'm afraid of you, not me." As if to make her point, she walked away from him and set her purse on the counter. It was then she spied the spread of food in her small kitchen.

"I am a man of my word, but you are tempted by what I can offer.

That is why you are afraid of yourself. You fear if you kiss me, you won't be able to stop there. I wouldn't blame you though."

She whirled and pinned her glare on him, wishing she could make him burst into flames. He mocked her. Insinuated she had no willpower and would simply fall under his spell. Well, Mia was no weakling. She'd already been on her own version of hell's rollercoaster and was still fighting her way back. If he thought to intimidate her, he was mistaken. Drawing her shoulders back, she marched to him. Stopped within inches of actual body contact, wrapped her arms around his neck then pulled him closer. Before she could chicken out, she planted her lips on his and upon contact realized what a grave error she had made.

He rested his palms on her hips but thankfully didn't tug her closer. His whiskers were surprisingly soft against her skin, and she found herself pressing into him. He parted his lips and his tongue swept out and caressed her own. She moaned and found herself opening to him.

What have I done?

CHAPTER EIGHT

HADES TASTED NOTHING BUT VANILLA. Sweet, rich vanilla with a hint of peach and it was the most decadent dessert that had ever laid across his tongue. All the willpower the god possessed was used to keep his hands from straying. From moving upward off her hips to her narrow waist and along her ribs until his palms met the soft flesh of her breasts. Instead, he remained steadfast. Hades never broke a vow, but at the moment, he wished he did as this was the perfect reason to do so.

With an erection pressing against his zipper, he did the only thing he could. Broke the kiss and stepped away. Mia stared at him as if he were crazy and he was. Crazy with desire for a human female and it made absolutely no sense to him. She wanted him, and he could have her if the desire swirling in her eyes was any indication of her state of mind. Now would be the time to strike and Mia wouldn't stop him.

She licked her lips and he nearly forgot his vow.

"Shall we dine?" He motioned to the table he had his minions bring in and set up. Mia followed his gaze and gasped.

"How did I miss that? I mean, I saw the food in the kitchen, but this..." She walked to the table and he was there ahead of her, pulling out a chair. She gave him a funny look but sat down.

Hades took the seat across from her, sent out a flare of power to dim the lights and ignite the candles both on the table and throughout the room. If the space didn't scream Christmas with the twinkling bulbs on the tree, flickering flames from dozens of candles, and the air filled with the scent of pine, then he was an utter failure.

"I just can't get over all the decorations." Mia inhaled. "What's for dinner? It smells so good."

He lifted the silver dome from the platter to reveal thick slices of perfectly pink prime rib of beef. "I hope you like a good chunk of meat."

Again, she swiped her tongue across her pink lips and this time he did groan.

"Something wrong?" She blinked in innocence. He found it hard to believe she had no idea what she did to a man.

"I find myself wanting to kiss you again, but this time I want to take my time and devour you."

Her cheeks flushed, and she glanced at the platter of meat. "Can I have that piece?" She pointed, obviously her plan was to ignore his remark.

Hades grabbed the fork and stabbed the beef. "You may have whatever you wish." Then placed it on her plate. He also scooped a spoonful of mashed potatoes and placed the mound next to the beef, followed by a hearty helping of green beans.

Mia held up her hand. "I'll start with this, thank you." Then dug in. Hades waited until she had her first bite of meat before he dished up his own food.

"Is it to your liking?" He sliced into the beef on his plate.

"Oh my god... I mean, wow it's so good."

He laughed. "Are you afraid to offend me by saying the word god?"

"Well, it does seem wrong," she answered between bites.

He waved her off. "Please, be yourself, Mia. The real you is much more pleasurable to be with than the fake one."

She stopped eating. "You think I'm fake?"

"I think you hide your true self. It's nothing more than a way to cope with what life has dealt you." He would be one to know, considering his own lot in life. "I've seen a glimpse of the woman inside you and I like her fire."

"My fire?" She raised a brow.

"Yes. I can't wait to see you in my world. I suspect you will become well respected by many if you show this same fire."

She played with her food and appeared in thought. "I'm not sure I understand." She glanced at the ticking clock on the wall when it struck.

"Do you worry about your curse?" He knew at the stroke of eleven her body would lose its mass and become nothing more than a ghost-like image.

"Will it make our trip difficult?" She had given up eating all together and this irritated him. "I mean I will be nothing more than a ghost at midnight when our bargain begins."

"Do not worry, Mia. It matters not what form your body is in when we depart." He wanted to assure her further, but a nagging pressure built in his temples.

What do you want, Zarek?

The shifter is in place and your presence required.

Hades threw down his napkin in disgust and rose from the table. "My dear Mia, I must beg your forgiveness. I'm afraid duty calls and I need to leave for a short time."

She jumped up. "Is everything okay?"

"It soon will be. I will be back by our agreed time." He didn't wait for further conversation but vanished and made his way to Vandeldor, where he found both Zarek and Argathos hiding in the shadows.

"She's over there," Zarek pointed out.

Hades followed and saw Leria staring at Aidyn from the shadows. Several shifters and vampires mingled around a large bonfire, while others sat at tables eating and drinking. All seemed oblivious to their surroundings except for two. Leria was also being watched by Aidyn. Matter of fact, the two appeared to be having a stare down when finally, the vampire king strode across the grounds.

Leria straightened, her right hand tucked into her flowing skirt, likely hiding the weapon Hades had given her. Heated words between the two that Hades didn't bother eavesdropping on were exchanged. He was more concerned with the time, ready for this to be over so he could return to his realm. Funny, not long ago he had threatened to stay in the human world, and now he couldn't wait to get back to Hell. Who would have thought he would be in such a hurry to re-enter his world? Certainly not him.

The scene unfolded in slow motion. Leria raised her arm and before Aidyn could react, the dagger of Embara was planted deep in his heart. The king stumbled backward, and it was Leria's own scream that broke through the chatter of partygoers. Men and women ran as the vampire king fell to the ground.

LERIA'S BLOOD-CURDLING scream pierced the night air, causing Lileta to drop the platter of food she'd been about to set on the table. Lileta searched through the crowd of people for the girl she and her mate Caleb had raised as their own daughter. When she managed her way through the people to stop beside Caleb, Lileta gasped. On the ground was the vampire king, a blade buried in his chest.

Marcus and his mate, Cassie, both healers, were on the ground next to Aidyn. Marcus pulled the blade from his king and paled.

"That's the blade of Embara," Seth shouted.

Everyone grew silent as they pinned their accusatory glares on a tearful Leria.

"Grab her," someone commanded.

Aidyn tried to sit up. "No."

Zarek stepped forward. When had he gotten here, Lileta

wondered, and why the hell didn't he do something? She moved to Leria and put her arm around the girl's shoulder.

"What is your dying wish?" Zarek directed his question at the vampire king.

"M-my mate... Clemency." Aidyn coughed blood and then the cold stare of death looked back at them all.

Marcus rose to his feet and faced Leria. "Did you kill the king?"

"I... He killed my father." She raised her chin, but Lileta sensed the uncertainty in the young woman. Leria had been struggling with many issues since she was a child. A young girl taken by Lowan and used as a pawn to make her father do the Dark Lord's bidding. When Odage had finally been caught, Aidyn had taken the dragon overlord into custody for the murder of the queen, Aidyn's mother. The punishment had been death, a bitter pill for Leria to swallow. Adding more tension to the situation, it was discovered that Leria and Aidyn were destined mates.

Why had fate been so cruel to bring these two to this crossroad?

"She killed the king. Punishment is death by your own law," Marcus growled, facing Zarek.

Lileta hugged Leria closer and Caleb stepped in front of them. Her strong, powerful mate would protect them both.

Bickering ensued until Zarek held up his hand. "Silence!" His command, followed by a burst of power, charged the air and promised pain to any who dared disobey.

"The king spoke his wish and it will be followed. Any of you who choose to harm the mate of the vampire king will suffer greatly."

"I can't imagine the pain you must feel right now. Your mate dead at your own hand," Cassie said. "Whatever issues the two of you had, I can't believe you really meant it to end like this."

"She is a murderer and does not deserve our mercy," a voice shouted.

"Disobey me and die," Zarek growled.

Caleb turned to Lileta. "Take Leria home. Now."

She didn't hesitate to remove herself and her daughter from the turbulent situation.

ONE WOULD HAVE THOUGHT her appetite might wane with the upcoming tick of the clock closing in on midnight. But Mia had nearly eaten herself into a coma. It was probably nerves. Maybe the good food. Most likely a combination of the most decadent food she had ever eaten and the fact she would soon be joining Hades in Hell. Was she more frightened of Hell or Hades? The man...err, god did something to her. His power frightened her. She had both seen him in action and felt the prickle of it across her skin. There was no doubt in her mind he could suck her soul out her nostril.

She wondered if that would hurt.

With a shiver, she forced her mind back to something else. Unfortunately, that something was how the god filled out a pair of jeans. The smoldering look he had given her earlier and the way he kissed. She touched her lips, still reeling from the claim he had made on them. How his hard body felt pressed against her own. That was where her real fear lie. How strong was her sexually deprived willpower? Could she spend thirty days in Hell with a man who was basically sex on two legs? Who no doubt knew his way around a woman's body like a pro. She reminded herself he promised to break her curse. They had both signed in blood the agreement and all he had asked of her was her company. Now, she wondered if she had read the contract thoroughly enough.

The clock struck on the eleventh bell. Her nightly curse took hold and ripped her world apart, reminding her of why she had made a deal with the god of the Underworld.

"Ugh! Why does this have to hurt so damn bad?" Her body contorted as it faded away and she became nothing more than a phantom. A woman without a physical body who floated across the room. At least now her gut no longer ached from overeating. That was some consolation. All she had to do now was wait another hour for Hades to show up. Would he come himself? Or, would he send one of his people like he had with the contract? She almost preferred the latter since she was in no rush to see the god of all evil again. Would her body—or lack thereof—still react to him in the same manner? Interesting thought and she had no idea what to expect.

Time always came to a screeching halt when she transformed. Probably because there was nothing to do. No sleep, no eating, or any of the normal things a person did. Her nightly escapades into the streets to try to help others came to an abrupt halt one night when she discovered an entire spooky-ass world out there. Saw the monsters that children feared under their bed. They were real. Very real indeed. Mia had been threatened by some shadowy monster that intended to cause her serious pain. Not knowing what else to do, she ran for her apartment and once inside discovered it was her sanctuary. Apparently, monsters couldn't enter where they were not invited. At least that seemed the case with the one who wanted to do vile things to her.

Finally, the clock began its loud chime, counting down until midnight and on the last stroke, tall, dark, and sexy as sin swirled into the room.

"Mia." He held out his hand.

"I can't take your hand." Was he daft? She wasn't able to touch solid objects, and unfortunately, Hades was about as solid as they came. So much for wondering if her ghostly libido would work. That sucker was kicking in full force.

He shook his head. Impatience drawn on his handsome features. "Trust me." He shoved his hand at her again.

With a sigh of aggravation, she laid her hand into his palm, and the second they made contact she returned to her corporeal self. "Holy shit!"

"As long as we stay physically connected, you will remain solid until we reach Hell."

Before she was able to respond, the room blurred then faded into blackness. Seconds later she wobbled, Hades' arm snaked around her waist to steady her and her feet were back on solid ground. She blinked and focused on the room surrounding her. Black floors with a sheen so high it was blinding. The walls were a deep red and reminded her of blood, and she suddenly had a vision of Hades' fangs deep in her neck. Chills ran up her spine. How could she even think of such a thing? *I must have been dropped on my head as a child.* It was the only explanation she could muster.

Hades looked at her and grinned. "Mia, I had no idea, but it would be my pleasure as well as yours to accommodate you."

Her jaw dropped open before she slammed it shut. "I... Stop reading my thoughts! It's rude."

He chuckled. "I find it most delightful. I am sorry, though, I really don't mean to do it. It's a habit that comes with being the god of Hell."

She could see where that might be true. After all, he would need to know who his enemies were in this world. She tried to forget her embarrassment by focusing on the throne at the end of the room.

"Dear god, is that your throne?"

"What? You don't like it?" To her relief, he released her and walked away. She glanced down at herself and held her hands out in front of her.

"You will remain corporeal while inside the palace. However, if you venture outside during your curse, I must admit I'm not sure what you'll become."

"Seriously?" The thought was rather frightening. "I'll be sure not to wander outside then." She had no desire to view Hell by herself anyway but wasn't ready to admit it.

Hades grabbed her by the shoulders and spun her to face him. Lines creased across his forehead and around those delectable lips. "You signed the contract agreeing to never leave the palace grounds without an approved escort."

"What if I break your rule? What do you intend to do to me?" Not sure why she goaded him.

"In this I will not waver. You will obey."

CHAPTER NINE

HADES NEARLY TREMBLED with fear and that never happened. Not in his entire existence had anything caused him to be afraid, but the thought of Mia stepping into his realm without him most certainly did. Perhaps bringing her here was a bad idea. Yet, he didn't want to send her home. Not yet at least. He was certain he would grow tired of her by the end of their agreed term.

"There are things out there, Mia, that you have no idea about. You are innocent and should not be subjected to them." His gaze grew heavy. "As for your punishment. I wouldn't hesitate to toss you over my knee for a good old-fashioned spanking." The thought sent all his blood straight to his dick. The blush across her cheeks didn't help either.

"I've seen evil things." She chewed her lip. "When I was cursed, it took me awhile to learn how to leave my apartment. One time I encountered something vile that frightened me so bad I ran back home. It wanted to harm me and thank god my apartment proved to be my sanctuary."

Every muscle in his body went rigid, and his temper reached a point that frightened even him. "What do you mean it meant you harm?" Somehow, he managed to at least keep his voice calm.

"It chased me and... I don't know but somehow it showed me visions of what it wanted to do to me." She rubbed her arms and Hades came unglued.

"What did this creature look like?" he demanded.

"A black shadow."

He recognized immediately what creature she described. It was known as a shadow demon and they were reputed for their nasty appetite. They could suck the life out of anything but only after they tortured the being to near madness. Mia now wore Hades' mark. A claim that she belonged to him and it was a brand that would be recognized by all of his minions. It was a claim he did not intend to remove even after he sent her home. It was the least she deserved. Some peace of mind that she would never again have to worry about creatures from the Underworld. What he would do is make sure the demon that dared frighten Mia was located. Hades would enjoy a little torture himself.

"Mia, you will not need worry about shadow demons or any others for that matter. Not while you wear my mark." His gaze flicked to her neck and he had the sudden desire to mark her there as well. Taste her skin as he sank his fangs into her throat and drank her essence. His cock responded to the vision in his head as did his fangs. Mia stared at him.

"Do you really use those things?" She was busy chewing her lip again.

"I do. Did you think they were for decoration?"

"You seriously drink blood? I guess that makes sense. I understand the guardians also drink blood and have been feeding off us without our knowledge forever. The thought that someone has bitten me, and I didn't even know it is a bit disturbing."

"You have not been bitten. I would see the markings." He closed the distance between them. "I would be your first and promise you would never forget it."

She stepped back, her eyes wide yet he didn't sense fear from her. "I'm sure it is an experience I'd remember and care not to." She touched her neck.

"Ah, Mia, yes, we can create extreme pain if we choose to. I can rip out the throat of even the most hardened demon. Yet, I can bring the greatest pleasure to those I wish to. You would only experience pleasure, that I promise."

"Why do you do this?"

"Do what? Be honest with you?"

"Can I see where I will be staying?"

The obvious quick change of subject told him all he needed to know. "How rude of me." He sent out a mental command to his favorite demon.

Baal, I need you to round up all the shadow demons for interrogation.

On it. Want to tell me what the fuck is going on with Aidyn?

We will discuss this later. He closed the connection and escorted Mia down the corridor.

MIA'S MIND whirled with thoughts that should probably be illegal or, at the very least, immoral. The sight of Hades sporting fangs was almost too much to bear. If she could kick her own ass she would because she didn't want to be imagining those points piercing her skin. Yet, it was all she could think about. She would never admit to wanting Hades in any way, shape, or form whatsoever. What she experienced was nothing more than what any woman would feel toward a handsome, viral man when she hadn't been laid in years. Part of her was like, *why not give him a go?* It would scratch an itch and Hades wouldn't be expecting a relationship that's for sure. She could have fun for the next thirty days then go back home and begin a normal life.

Easy peasy.

Except something held her back. She forced her focus to the brightly lit corridor Hades led her down.

"I have to admit, I imagined this place to be much darker than it is."

"Why? Because it's Hell?" He sounded offended and that was not her intention.

"Sorry, but yeah."

"Parts of Hell are actually quite beautiful. However, there are areas that are what you'd expect." He stopped in front of an oversized, black door. "This is your chamber." He pushed open the door and waited for her to walk inside.

Offering him a glance, she stepped in and looked around. A large sitting room with a loveseat and two chairs that looked as if they might swallow her up in their cushy comfort faced a fireplace. The walls—unlike the corridor—were a warm vanilla and the artwork that of beautiful landscapes. There was a small kitchenette that housed a fridge and microwave, and when she opened the fridge, she was surprised to see bottles of water, juice, and all kinds of meats and cheese. There was enough in there to take care of any midnight munchie attack.

Moving on, she entered the bedroom where she found a king-size bed and visions of what she could do with the man following her popped into her head.

Damn it! She ignored the thoughts and walked straight to the bathroom where a shower done in black and gold tile was at least three times larger than her entire bathroom back home. Mia wasn't even going to allow her mind to go there. Instead, she whirled around and headed back through the bedroom where—lord have mercy—Hades was stretched out on her bed. The white shirt he'd been wearing seemed to have unbuttoned itself. Her heart beat faster and her cheeks so hot she swore the heat in the room had been turned up several degrees.

"What the ever-loving hell?" She crossed her arms over her chest. Told herself it was to show her anger when in reality she needed to make sure he didn't see her nipples were trying to tear through her shirt. They wanted his lips wrapped around them, and she wanted to scream in frustration.

He raised a brow in question. "What? I thought I'd take a rest while you mill about." He sat up and swung his legs to the edge of the bed. The shirt she now noticed was not only unbuttoned but pulled free of his slacks. It fell open to reveal the peaks and valleys of hard muscles she had always known were there.

"You swore you would not do this."

"I have done nothing, Mia. It is you who stammer about and refuse to admit what your body craves." He rose to his full height and her gaze did a slow, lazy scan downward. The god was nothing but sin. Dark, dangerous, sinful and hell if she didn't want to find out how naughty he really was.

"You are the most arrogant ass I've ever met."

"Of course, I am. I'm Hades. I thought we had already established that I am not your average man." He sauntered. No, he prowled like the dangerous predator he was, closer to her until she had to take a step back. She bumped something and could go no farther unless she turned and ran. No way was she backing down.

"We had a deal. You would not expect sex from me while I was here."

"And I am a god of my word. Have I spoken anything of sex?" He was so close now his spicy scent wrapped around her and nearly caused her to moan out loud.

"You use other methods to get your point across." She slammed her hands on her hips and leaned forward. "And I thought I established that Hell would have to freeze over before I ever slept with you."

He gave a sexy grin that always undid her. A hint of fang peeked over his full lips. "I can make that happen, Mia. I *can* make Hell freeze over." He stepped back and slowly began to fade. "Breakfast is in an hour. I expect you to dress accordingly to sit at my table." Then he was gone.

She released her breath. Thankful he had the sense to leave because she had been on the verge of caving. This was going to be the longest thirty days of her life.

HADES FLOATED AWAY LAUGHING and headed to his suite across from Mia's. He would have loved to stick around longer and torture her into submission, but he was in need of a shower. He couldn't remember the last time he had felt so invigorated. So alive. He was going to enjoy his new guest's stay, and he would one day soon savor those well-toned thighs wrapped around his waist.

He stripped and headed for his own bathroom when a disturbance filled the room.

"For fuck's sake, I did not want to see your bare ass," Baal said.

"Well, then you should knock first." Hades summoned a silk robe. "You have the demons I asked for?"

"Yes, and all are quaking in their shadows when I told them Hades had requested an audience up close and personal." He grew serious. "It didn't take long for Lowan and his lackeys to begin their holy terror on humanity."

Hades sighed. "How bad is it?"

"Well, no worse than before I guess. People seemed to be expecting it and were prepared." Baal crossed his arms. "It appears that several were lining up to have Aidyn turn them into vampire warriors, but there seems to be a bit of a problem."

"What's that?"

His brows dipped. "The fucking vampire king was stabbed by his mate with the blade of Embara. Something tells me you knew that already."

Hades walked to his bar and poured a whiskey. "I knew. I'm the one who gave her the dagger."

"What the fuck is wrong with you?" Baal yelled.

Hades sipped, allowing the heat of the alcohol to burn his throat. Maybe it would deflate his dick. "I do not like your tone."

Baal pulled in a breath and released it slowly. "Sorry, my lord. But I think you owe me an explanation as to why my best friend was murdered."

"It's simple. Aidyn is really the Phoenix god and his death was necessary to force him to rise again."

"The fuck you say?" Baal scratched his chin. "Shouldn't that be happening soon? And why doesn't anyone else know this?"

Hades shrugged. "We've no idea how long it will take. I was the only one who knew who Pyros really was. Only recently did Zarek and Argathos find out."

"You mean you've known all this time? In the meantime, everyone wants to kill Leria for murdering the king. Did she know?"

"No." He waved Baal off. "She was simply a means to an end is all."

"So, you come back here to play with your new female while everyone waits for the other boot to drop?" He shook his head. "Why am I not surprised?"

"Where is the king now?" Hades grew tired of going toe-to-toe with his commander. He had better things to do.

"I understand Zarek took the body back to Katie's."

"Perfect. Now, run along. I have important things to do, like attend the rise of my brother." He dismissed Baal and went to take his shower. After eating, he would be paying a visit to his niece and to hell with the rules Zarek had laid down. It was time for a change.

CHAPTER TEN

MIA CLEANED up and went through the closet only to discover that if Hades expected her to keep all of the items inside it, she would need a new apartment. Correction, an entire house wouldn't be big enough. She would simply have to select her favorites and be content with that. As she stared in the mirror, she was certain there would be no place back home to wear the getup she had put on. A red sheath dress that she had to practically pour herself into. Granted, it covered her ass and breasts. Barely. But damn, even she had to admit she had never looked so good.

Finally deciding she was ready, she walked from her room and was greeted in the corridor by Hades. He sported a dark gray suit and a blue shirt. It brought out his new eye color. She still didn't understand the transformation but secretly loved the new look. The god had been hot before, but now he was one smoldering, sinful male specimen that put all others to shame. As he smiled and offered his arm, she would do well to remind herself that he was Hades, god of the Underworld, and way the hell out of her league.

"That dress suits you," he purred.

"Hmm. I will admit I feel rather naughty wearing it." Even more so with the three-inch open toe heels she'd slipped on. Funny how clothing really did empower a girl.

"I think I like the naughty Mia. Are you hungry?"

"Actually, I am. I do hope you are not serving goat's head or anything like it."

He laughed. "You are a treasure, and no. You will find breakfast to be made up of food I promise you can identify."

"Good. I really didn't want to starve to death while here."

They continued their walk through a large open breezeway. Marble columns arched on both sides of them and framed gardens filled with things she would expect to see back home. Bushes trimmed so not even a sprig was out of place.

"Are those roses?"

"Yes. Perhaps after we eat, you'd care for a tour of the gardens? We grow spectacular roses."

"I would. Yes." So, Hell had flowers. Who knew?

He escorted her to a table that must have seated at least twenty people and there were already three seated. When they arrived, everyone stood and gave Hades a bow.

"My lord," they said in unison and Mia became a bit uncomfortable.

Hades had never mentioned anything about formalities. Did he expect her to follow? Shit, how did one treat a god? For some reason, it wasn't until now—when she bore witness to how others reacted—that she gave it much thought.

"Everyone, this is Mia and she will be our guest for the next thirty days. You will treat her with the same respect given to me." He glared at each one before bringing his gaze back to her. "Mia, this is Aster." He motioned to the drop-dead gorgeous woman to his left. Mia shifted, now uncomfortable in her skin-tight dress and heels.

"Next to Aster is Lilona."

Another stunning female and Mia wanted to crawl under the table. These women dripped sex appeal, and she suddenly wondered if Hades was sleeping with them. Both women offered her a smile that spoke volumes. They simply had to be Hades' mistresses.

"To your right is my highest-ranking officer, Baal. He tends to all my personal matters as well as commands my army, but I didn't think he would be joining us for brunch. It's most unusual."

"Mia, it is a pleasure to meet you. Please excuse my curiosity, it's not often Hades has guests such as yourself." He bent at the waist, took her hand, and placed a soft kiss on her knuckles. "My lady."

"Thank you. It's nice to meet all of you."

Hades pulled out her chair and waited for her to sit.

"Thank you." She took her seat then Hades moved to the highback to her left at the head of the table. Once he was seated, everyone else took their place again. Soon the room was bustling with well-dressed men carrying silver trays. Her cup was filled with coffee and crystal glasses of water and orange juice set before her. Platters of fruit and various breads were also set out and a man stopped next to her.

"My lady, how shall we prepare your meal today?"

She looked up. "Uh." Then glanced around. Hades was busy chatting with Aster and Lilona when Baal leaned in.

"They will make you whatever you wish. Think of it like a restaurant without a menu. Your choices are limitless."

"Thank you," she whispered. "I would like a spinach omelet with feta cheese and a side of bacon, please."

"Right away, my lady." The man gave a slight bow and scurried off.

Mia leaned closer to Baal, thankful for his assistance. "Thanks again. I feel like such a nit-wit."

"Anytime." He passed a platter of rolls and breads which she accepted. Plucking off a muffin that looked like cranberry, she hoped her guess was correct.

"So, you are Hades' right-hand man?" She pulled apart her muffin and took a small bite, relieved it was indeed cranberry and the best damn muffin ever!

"I am. I had hoped my mate might be able to join us, but she got tied up with business. You would like Ranata, perhaps she can visit while you're here."

"Is she a demon too? I...uh might be assuming too much to think you are?" Awkward!

He laughed. "While I am demon, my beautiful mate is not. She is half human and half fae. A queen of her people, hence the important business."

"Oh." She really had no idea what to say. There was so much in the world she didn't understand.

"Mia, darling," Aster spoke up. "If Hades approves, I would love to show you around the finer areas of Hell."

Now that was a surprise. Aster struck her as the kind of woman who would find such a task beneath her. Had Hades put her up to it? The two had been talking in hushed tones after all.

"That is very kind of you. I would love to." She looked to Hades for disapproval, considering he had been the one to tell her she wasn't to leave the grounds without an approved escort.

"I will provide a list of places you may escort Mia to. Thank you, Aster."

Well, so much for that idea. Guess she would be spending time with the... Hell, she didn't even know what Aster was.

"I'll tag along," Lilona said.

Oh, goody. Mia would have to make it clear she had no dibs on Hades. Last thing she wanted was a cat fight with these two.

HADES TOOK Mia on a quick tour of the gardens before he excused himself. "I'm sorry, but I have some important business I need to tend to. However, Baal here would be happy to show you around the rest of the grounds while I'm away. I hope not to be gone long."

"I don't want to be a burden. I'm sure Baal has better things to do than babysit me."

"Nonsense. He will do whatever I tell him and be happy about it." He glanced at Baal. "Right?"

"Of course, my lord. Don't I always?" Baal smirked.

"Usually with much bitching." He brought his focus back to Mia. He really did love the way she looked in the red dress. His taste in clothing was impeccable and he couldn't wait to see her in every item. She had thought to thwart him by demanding her body be completely covered, but little did she realize how sexy she was even if her breasts were not hanging out. It simply went to prove she didn't understand the male mind. He was quite capable of imagining what lay beneath that dress.

"I will be back soon, and when I am, it will mean my brother has risen." He vanished, sorry to leave Mia but knew she was in good hands. Baal would protect her with his life if called on. Hades doubted there would be any trouble, most feared him but there were a few who could get some bright idea that harming Mia might be a way to break Hades. Little did they know he was unbreakable.

Appearing in the middle of the courtyard at the palace where Katie and Seth now lived, it seemed he had come just in time. He strode forward. Aidyn lying on the stone slab, flames circling him, was the center of attention.

"I can't fucking believe it," Marcus said from next to Hades.

He simply grinned. "Believe it. My brother has been closer than any of you realized for centuries waiting to awaken."

"You knew?" Cassie asked.

"I've always known."

Zarek and Argathos moved closer to Hades and he knew it was time. The three gods walked through the fire—whispers came from behind them—until they stood directly at the altar. Each laid a hand on the slain king.

"Brother, we have waited far too long for you to return to us," Zarek said.

"It is time for you to awaken," Argathos spoke.

Hades choked back emotion. He had missed his brother probably more than the others. He and Pyros had always been close. More like their father than the other two and they understood each other. Hades would be glad to have his brother back in his life.

"Brother, the pieces are falling into place. Your resurrection will line the stars so the one who is destined to end this madness will be unshackled," Hades said.

The fire roared around them in response. Blue flame mingled with the red-orange and consumed the body of Aidyn. Seconds ticked before the guardian king sat up and stared down his brothers.

My mate, I will be back for her. He sent the mental message to his brothers right before he shifted into the bird of the Phoenix and launched into the sky. The ring of fire trailed behind him and everything fell silent until finally Katie spoke up.

"So, where did he go?"

"Son of a bitch. I would have never suspected Aidyn was the Phoenix god," Marcus said. "What now?" There was no mistaking the pain in the warriors' voice. Marcus had been Aidyn's protector and closest friend.

Hades understood the meaning behind the question, but it was not up to him to respond. "Pyros or, as you know him, Aidyn has gone somewhere to be alone while he finishes regenerating. It could be days, weeks, or months. We have no way to know."

"He will be back and continue to be your king, of that I am sure," Zarek offered. "He's still the same man you have come to respect and love over the centuries. There's simply more to him now." He moved away from the altar. "It is time for your savior to be set free and begin preparations to remove Lowan for good. Many things still need to happen before Pyros comes back to hand off his dagger one last time."

"Who the hell is this person that will shove that blade into Lowan's chest?" Lucan had finally made his presence known.

"She is your mate, Lowan's sister Sabin. And before she can commit her act of betrayal against her own brother, she needs your darkness. You need to rescue her and get this mating process completed," Hades stated.

"Well, aren't we just all royally fucked. If you think I'm mating with our enemy's sister, then you are crazier than I imagined." Lucan moved closer. "Not to mention, why should we trust her? She is, after all, the sister of your crazy-ass grandson."

MIA WAS SLIGHTLY PUT out by Hades' hasty retreat, but there was nothing to be done about it. "So... Here we are."

"I sense this entire situation makes you uncomfortable," Baal said. "I get it. Hell can be rather intimidating to those who have never been here before." He grinned. "Look on the bright side, at least you're not here to be tortured."

Well, she wasn't too sure about that. Sometimes, looking at Hades was its own torture. To her body at least. "True."

"Let's walk. I'll show you the rest of the estate." The demon led her under an archway covered in blood-red roses and into an open, grassy area.

"Wow. If I didn't know better, I'd think I was back home." She admired the rolling hills until her eye caught a large building. "What's that?" She pointed.

"That would be the stables."

She whipped her head around so fast her curls smacked her in the face. "What?"

The look on her face must have been priceless because Baal broke out laughing. "Yes, Hades has horses."

Mia had gone riding a few times when she was a child. It was a fond memory of time spent with her brother and she had fallen in love with the majestic creatures. Unfortunately, life had never given her another opportunity to go riding again. "Can I see them?"

"Sure." His gaze ran down her tight dress and to her heels. "Though I don't think you want to walk across the field in that getup." He offered his arm. "Take my arm and I will save us the hike."

She hesitated only a moment. Unsure if it was wise but then her curiosity won out and she laid her hand on his forearm. Instantly, everything went black before it became bright again and they were standing inside the stable. Mia inhaled the scent of fresh straw. Glancing around, her gaze fell on the most majestic beast she had ever seen.

She stepped closer to the stall.

"Careful. Phantom is Hades' personal steed and moody as fuck. He usually doesn't like strangers."

"He is beautiful." The horse towered over her but dipped his head over the stall door as if reaching out. She stepped closer. Unable to resist the horse that was dark as a moonless night. Not a speck of color to be found. Even his eyes were like coal. "I can see how he comes by his name." She reached out and touched his nose.

"Ha! He doesn't get the name Phantom from his color. He is a true steed of Hell and more demonic than me."

"Seriously?" She hardly believed it. The animal responded to her touch by pressing his enormous head into her hand. She laughed. "Are you an attention hound?"

"Hades' steed never lets anyone touch him except for Hades," Aster said behind them.

Mia and Baal both turned.

"He must like you," she continued. Mia noticed the female was dressed in jeans, a blouse, and boots.

"I take it you ride?"

"I do. I like to take Damon out when I can. He's a very spirited animal. What about you, do you ride?"

"It was a long time ago, but I enjoyed it thoroughly." She was so out of her league here. Maybe it would be better if she just went back and hid in the palace until Hades returned.

"You should come with me. Perhaps tomorrow." Aster smiled.

"We can ride the grounds. I'm sure there is a horse here that would be suitable."

Mia glanced at Baal, who shrugged. Well, that wasn't much help.

"I would like that."

Aster gave a firm nod. "It's a date then. After breakfast?"

"Sounds good." Hopefully there was some suitable clothing in that monstrosity of a closet. She'd have to make sure and check when she got back. She gave Phantom one last scratch.

"Shall we finish our tour, or would you like to go back?"

"I think I've seen enough for one day." She was ready to slip into something more her style and the heels—as nice as they were—were murder on her feet.

CHAPTER ELEVEN

HADES WAS anxious to return home, which surprised him greatly. After centuries of being confined, he thought having freedom would be the most important thing. However, it appeared Mia intrigued him more than he had anticipated. He found he enjoyed spending time with her and wanted to share his world. It was likely his brother wouldn't be back for some time. It was also just as likely there would soon be chaos in Hell when Lucan went to rescue Sabin. Oh sure, the vampire was in complete denial that she was his mate, or he would be claiming her at this very moment. They'd all seen this scene play out before with Marcus, Seth, and even Caleb. All three men had tried with great difficulty to keep from claiming their mates.

All had failed miserably.

"I must return home." He also hadn't forgotten he was still under his eldest brother's keep. Unable to travel to the human realm unless summoned.

Zarek strode to him. "Before you go, I will have a word."

Hades didn't stop from rolling his eyes. "Must we do this now?"

"I command it as your king."

"Fucking king card. I suppose next you'll want me to kneel and kiss your boots?" he growled. Before he was able to take in another breath, he was transported against his will only to find himself suddenly seated at a table. He looked around and recognized the room to be in Zarek's own palace. A stunning redhead came running at him.

"Hades!"

Hades rose and pulled his sister-in-law into an embrace. "Qadira, love. Has my brother been good to you?"

She gave him a kiss on the cheek. "I manage to keep him in line." She laughed, and they broke free when Zarek cleared his throat.

"My wife manages to keep me on my toes," Zarek said.

Hades winked. "Good girl."

"I will leave you two to whatever business you have." She touched Hades on the arm. "I've missed you, please don't be a stranger."

Hades gave a nod. He remembered when his brother had fallen for the goddess of fire and creator of dragons. It had been a whirlwind affair with Zarek being smitten to the core. The goddess was good for all of them, but Hades would freely admit to being jealous of what Zarek had. He'd also seen the other side of what could happen when Argathos had fallen apart when his own wife had been murdered. It was what had started the war that had caused them all to flee their home world and start again. It was why Hades had been condemned to be the punisher of evil.

"So, what is it you want from me now?" Hades didn't bother to hide his sarcasm.

"You know, you only had to ask me, and I would have allowed you your freedom."

The snarl started as a small quiver of his lower lip, and his nostrils flared before he curled his lip to reveal his fangs. "You arrogant fuck." He jumped out of his chair so fast it flew backward and splintered into several pieces. He would have to remember to make his apologies to Qadira after he kicked his brother's ass.

In seconds, he had fistfuls of Zarek's shirt and the bastard brother within inches of him. "I do not beg. Ever!"

Zarek's power flared around him and sent bolts through Hades until he was no longer able to hold on. With a growl, he let go and stepped back. Prepared to unleash his own fury.

"I never asked you to beg. Simply ask like any decent being, but I forgot you have no decency. It's why I condemned you and your dark fucking soul."

Every muscle went taut and in that twinkle of time, he wanted nothing more than to bring his brother to his knees. Make him beg for mercy so Hades could refuse to give it. He had the power to do it. Hades had harnessed all the power of Hell, and his big brother the king was unaware that his shitty little brother could indeed rip apart the universe. Blast every living being into oblivion. For a brief moment the darkness swelled inside him. Threatened to spill like a thick, inky sludge until it drowned everything in its stickiness of evil. He must have allowed a glimpse of power to flare beneath the surface because for a second, Zarek's eyes widened before the god regained his composure.

"I never should have given you dominion over evil," Zarek said.

Hades fought to remain in control. Visions of Mia filled his head and soothed him until he was able to pull himself from the darkness. He took a deep breath. "Unlike Father, I have control of myself."

Zarek gave a nod. "That is a good thing because the reason I called you here was to tell you that I have removed all barriers between you and the human realm as well as here. You may come and go at your will. Your home here among us awaits you should you choose to accept it."

Hades was momentarily shocked. Had he heard his brother correctly? "What is the catch?" There was always a string attached to anything his older brother—the king—did. Not that Hades blamed him. It was also how he operated.

"No catch. It is time for you to come home. You have proven your ability to control your power."

"What about Hell? I should simply leave it?"

Zarek summoned two glasses of wine and offered one to Hades. "It is your realm and will always remain so. You have a powerful army. Baal is most competent to keep the place civil when you are not there. Live between the two as you see fit."

For once in his life Hades was speechless. Wasn't this what he had always wanted? Now that it was offered to him, he wasn't so sure. He had grown used to the darkness, but he imagined Mia gracing the rooms of his palace here among the gods. He shook the image free. Hades would have Mia, and then she would become a distant memory like all the others.

Zarek raised his glass. "To my brother finally coming home."

Hades raised his as well and gave a nod. "To coming home."

MIA HAD BEEN in Hell for exactly one week. She and Aster had gone riding twice and she enjoyed it thoroughly. Part of her daily routine now consisted of paying a visit to the stables and spending time with Phantom. She was growing quite fond of the horse and the beast seemed to reciprocate.

Hades spent most of his days busy with whatever an evil god did but was always there for breakfast and dinner. She should be grateful he was otherwise occupied. It helped keep her hormones in check. Today however, he was taking her on her first trip outside his compound. She was careful to dress in jeans and a tee as well as tennis shoes. Comfort as well as staying covered up was important.

As she made her way down the stairs, she contemplated how to approach a question that had been nagging at her since she'd arrived. When she reached the last step, Hades was there to greet her. It was totally unfair that he looked just as sexy in jeans as he did in a suit.

"Shall we?" He offered his arm.

"Okay." She wrapped her fingers around his bicep and nearly

groaned on contact with the thick, hard muscle. Mia couldn't escape Hell fast enough with her promise to not cave into sex with the god.

He led her out of the palace and along a stone path. They walked several minutes in silence, which was unusual for Hades.

"You are quiet today," she said.

"I'm sorry. Please excuse my bad manners."

Now she knew something was wrong. Even though she hadn't been around the god much, she had been enough to read his moods. "Care to talk about it?"

He glanced at her. "My shoulders are big. There is no need for you to carry my burdens."

His comment had her wanting to help him carry that weight. "Hades, no one should go it alone. Not even the god of the Underworld."

He stopped several yards from a wrought-iron gate and faced her. It was then she noticed his eyes matched Hell's sky. Both were so intense she gasped.

"What?" He looked around as if to locate a threat.

"Your eyes have changed color again. They are the same blue as the sky."

"Seems since I have met you many things about me have changed."

"Is that what's bothering you?"

He shook his head. "No, but it looks as if my eldest brother has lifted my curse. The one that has kept me locked away here unless summoned."

"But that's wonderful!" Wasn't it?

"He has also given me back my home."

"Your home?" Now she was utterly confused.

He started to walk again. "Yes. All of the gods have a home in a place called the Temple of the Gods. I haven't seen mine since I was condemned to the Underworld."

This time she stopped and forced him to look at her. "How long have you been here?"

He gave a half-hearted smile. "It has been so long I hardly remember. Since I was a young god." There was no mistaking the pain in his eyes that flashed away seconds later.

"Can I ask how old you are now?" She hoped it wasn't impolite to pose the question.

He ignored her by turning away and started walking again. They finished the journey through an iron gate that—to her surprise—was only guarded by two men she assumed to be demons. Once they were on the other side, she was met by an endless sea of nothing. The ground under her was covered by crushed rocks as black as a crow's wing. The sun bore down on them with such intensity she swore her skin would melt away from her bones at any moment. Sweat beaded and made its way into places that had her shifting her stance.

"This, Mia, is true Hell. An ocean of nothing. No shade. No water. No life. It's simply void of anything more than rock and heat."

She turned and looked around. "Where is the gate?" Everything was gone.

"It's still there, but you can no longer see it. This is true purgatory."

She swallowed. "I thought Hell was full of screaming souls being tortured." She shook her head in disbelief at what lay before her compared to the vision her mind had always held.

"Can you imagine roaming this for eternity? Your soul forever stuck here?"

She shivered despite the overbearing heat. "No."

He faced her. "I was sent here when I was one hundred. To a human that would equal a teenager. I am now two hundred thousand years old."

She tried to swallow the gasp, but it escaped anyway.

"Yes, that is a long time. Time to learn how to control my power and turn this place into something more. Time to be forever alone." With that he waved his hand and the transformation in front of her was monumental.

The air cooled to a more comfortable temperature. Green

covered the ground in the form of thick, lush grass. She noted houses also dotted the landscape and people seemed to be out socializing like any small neighborhood might.

"What just happened?" She hadn't forgotten the last comment he'd made about being alone. There was no way to fathom how long he had actually been alive and forced to live in this purgatory.

"That, my dear Mia, is the power of a god. For those deserving, I can change the landscape to something more fitting. Something more tolerable."

"Damn." That was some power indeed.

"I can transform Hell at a whim to whatever I wish. Some areas are as you would expect with the screaming, tortured souls."

She dug for the courage to ask the burning question. "What did you mean by being alone? There seems to be plenty of people… ummm, demons around you."

"When you are the most powerful being in a world, enemies pretend to be your friend. Everyone has a motive, and no one is to be trusted."

It suddenly hit her like a load of bricks. She was able to clearly see how Hades might be treated by those around him. It would be like suddenly winning the lottery. You would have no idea who to trust. She squared her shoulders. "Hades, you can trust me."

His gaze narrowed. "Is that so? Even you want something from me. To free you from your curse so you may live a normal life."

"I did, but we made a deal. In return for your favor, I agreed to come here. You can read me, this I know, so you can see my intentions."

He studied her for a moment. "Yes. Your intentions are clear. It is what attracts me to you. You are the only being who has no ulterior motive against me. You don't wish for my kingdom or my power. Nor do you want to be lavished in riches. You are truly unique. I am humbled that you allow me to share my world with you."

"No, Hades. It is I who am humbled."

HADES BECAME A MAN OBSESSED. Fading everything around them into the background, he hid them from any prying eyes as he bent down, cupped Mia's cheeks, and leaned in to kiss her. He was positive when he lay claim to her mouth, she would recoil even though deep down she desired him. However, to his surprise, she softened into him. Parted her lips, her tongue darting out to meet his. The intimate contact sent heated blood coursing through his veins and straight to his now thickening shaft. He should break away, yet he was unable. Truth be told, he didn't want to.

A sexy mewl came from the female in his embrace, and her kiss deepened as she slipped her arms around his waist. Vanilla consumed all of his senses and nearly sent him to his knees. Finally, he pulled himself from the lust he was drowning in and broke the kiss. Mia looked at him, eyes filled with desire and breaths coming in heavy pants.

"I would apologize, but I am not sorry. You do something to me that no other ever has. I don't pretend to understand it, but I made a vow to you and intend to keep it." He stepped back and scrubbed his palm down his face. "In order for me to remain a man of my word, I must send you home."

Her eyes widened. "But—"

He held up a hand. "I will break your curse, Mia, and you can go home at the end of the week. If you stay any longer, I will forget my vow and I *will* have you in my bed."

"Oh." Her voice so soft had he not been an immortal with perfect hearing he may have missed it. There was also no denying the disappointment in her eyes. If Mia really wanted him, she would come to him. She had until the end of the week. Five long agonizing days to say she wanted him in her bed.

"We should head back. I have things to do." Namely remove himself from the presence of the female in front of him.

CHAPTER TWELVE

MIA'S BODY did a fast furious burn and every nerve was hypersensitive. There was no doubt if Hades rubbed his thumb across her aching nipples, she would immediately come undone. Why did her body betray her like this? Of course, the god was sex and sin rolled into one scrumptious package. Any woman with eyes would desire him. Not to mention he smelled like Heaven even though Hell ran through his veins. There was more to him, however. Mia had seen the flash of loneliness and pain in his eyes. There was no fathoming what it must be like to live in an eternal hell for as long as he had.

Two hundred thousand years.

Her heart shattered for the man whose own brothers had condemned him to such a fate. Now, he rejected her, but it was out of fear. He so much as admitted he wanted her, and it was why he was sending her home. Part of her wanted to rebel against the idea. Yet, Mia wasn't a one-night stand kind of girl, and no matter how much she wanted him, she wanted a broken heart even less. She wasn't foolish enough not to realize there was no way they could ever be any more than lovers for a brief period. He was a freaking god after all and she a mere mortal.

"Hades?" she spoke as they walked back to the palace.

"What is it?"

"After you lift my curse and I go back home, will I still wear your mark?"

"Yes. It will keep you safe until this war with Lowan is over. After that I will remove it."

Disappointment came over her. He was going to break all ties and she should be pissed as hell at him for stringing her on. Should be elated to be rid of Hades, god of the Underworld. Yet, she felt neither.

"Will we still remain friends?"

He glanced at her, surprise in his eyes. "You wish to be my friend?" Was that hope in his voice?

Her heart broke again. "You said yourself I have no ulterior motive. Yes, I want to be your friend."

He didn't look at her again, only kept walking. "Perhaps."

Silence filled the thick air until they reached the palace where Hades left her in the den. "Tonight after dinner, I will remove your curse."

"What about our contract?"

"I will void it, but you may still take the clothing as promised."

Before she was able to respond, he was gone, and she was left standing alone until Aster pulled her from her thoughts.

"Mia, darling, I expected you to be gone for hours." She had slipped in behind Mia and Lilona stood next to her. Both women wore jeans and a top cut so low there was nothing left to the imagination. Mia had recently learned during the time spent with Aster that both women were what was known as a succubus. Female demons who required sex to survive. It was evident they were part of Hades' harem of females. Mia liked Aster, yet a tinge of jealousy crept over her.

"Hades had business, so we came back early."

"For shame. Listen, there is a party later this week and we would love to take you."

"I'll be going home at the end of the week." The words nearly choked her.

"But I thought you were here for an entire month?" Lilona asked, a pout on her mouth. Normally the woman was quiet, and Mia had rarely seen her except for meal times.

"Appears not." She didn't feel like going into details. "You ladies heading out?"

Aster grinned. "Yes. Lilona and I are going to one of the local clubs for some much-needed sex."

Mia admired the other woman's openness and how she owned her sexuality. Perhaps there was something to be learned. "Well, good luck. I'll see you later. Maybe?" She smiled and headed upstairs, feeling the need for a shower.

Several hours and a nap later, a knock came at her bedroom door. Dropping the book she had been reading, Mia opened the door to find one of Hades' helpers on the other side.

"My lady." He gave a bow and held out a silver tray holding an ivory envelope. "Hades has asked me to deliver this to you."

"Thank you." She took the paper and closed the door, preparing herself for the worst. Hades had never sent a note to her before, and she only imagined it was more bad news. Pulling the paper from its sealed envelope, she found a thick ivory card that read.

MY DEAREST MIA,

I WOULD BE PLEASED if you joined me for dinner tonight in a very special place. Please wear a gown of your choice. I will send someone to escort you promptly at 7:00 pm.

Hades

. . .

MIA HELD the note to her chest. "A special place?" Where was he taking her and why now? Was it because her time here was almost over? She recalled his words from earlier in the day and suddenly had an idea. Glancing at the clock, she had exactly two hours to get ready. Not nearly enough time, but she would have to make do.

Running to the closet, she whipped open the double doors and stepped inside. To the left were all the gowns. More than twenty and she was going to go through every single one until she found the sexiest of them all. As she grabbed the first, a black one that covered her entire chest, she cursed her request for coverage and now wished for less. Tossing the dress aside, she pushed each gown across the metal rod, rejecting them all until she came to a deep purple gown made of soft silk. The bodice was a combination of lace and silk arranged in a floral display.

She pulled it off the hanger and moved to the full-length mirror, holding the gown in front of her. "Nice." She laid the dress on the bed then stripped. With great care, she pulled the gown over her head and down her hips until it settled into a sweep of fabric at her feet.

"Wow." She stared at herself. The floral lace covered her breasts yet left enough to offer any man a glimpse that would make him beg for more. A slit up the front showed more thigh than her shorts usually did. The dress was amazing but now for her hair and makeup.

Mia was careful with the application of makeup. She was never one who wore a lot, but tonight she applied all of the basics and even managed to pull off a smoky eye. The last thing was lip color followed by gloss. As she stepped away, applying final touches to her hair which she had decided to leave down, she was stunned by her own appearance.

Hades wouldn't know what hit him.

As she slipped on her heels, a knock came at the door. Time to go wow the lord of Hell.

HADES STOOD at the railing and stared over the vast gardens. Every flower known to mankind and some that were his own creation were in bloom and fragranced the air. It was the delicate step of female heels that caught his attention and drew him away from the place that was often his only escape. Turning, his breath was pulled from his lungs as he stared at Mia. He had thought the gown exceptional when he'd chosen it and he had been correct.

Her escort gave a bow and backed away as Mia continued toward him. A grin on her lips that indicated she knew exactly what the sight of her did to him. He was angry with himself for not escorting her. How could he have allowed her to walk through the palace dressed to kill?

"Mia. You are stunning." He swept forward and placed a kiss on her cheek.

"Thank you. I must admit, I had fun dressing up."

He offered his arm and walked to the table where the glasses of Champagne already waited. "You have never had the opportunity to be so extravagant." There was no missing the flush to her cheeks under Hell's moonlight.

"No. While my family didn't lack for anything, parties where we dressed up like this"—she gave the dress a swirl—"didn't ever happen. I must admit, I feel like a princess."

It brought him great joy to hear her say that. "You wear the color of royalty. Did you know that?"

She glanced down at herself. "I never thought about it when I picked the dress." Her gaze met his and it was full of determination.

He handed her a glass and raised his for a toast. "To Hell's new princess. You bring a much-needed beauty to this place."

"Thank you." She sipped her Champagne. "So, why are we having this fancy evening?"

He didn't dare tell her that he wanted her all to himself. Even after his earlier confession that he couldn't be near her, he found he couldn't stay away either. "I thought it might be nice to share an evening without the others." Mostly true.

"I see." She looked upward. "It's hard to believe one is in Hell with such a beautiful full moon. The thing is huge!"

He had made it so, just for her. Knowing how beautiful she would look under its bright light. "It lights the garden and lake very well."

"There's a lake?"

He smiled. "This is my favorite place. Unlike the gardens you toured earlier, this is my private sanctuary. No one but I am allowed here."

"I see."

"I would be honored to share it with you. Dinner will be ready when we are. Shall we walk first?"

"I would love to. Fill my glass though?" She held out the crystal flute.

Hades pulled the bottle from the ice bucket and refilled both their glasses. He then led Mia down the few stairs to a stone path. On either side roses reached out and perfumed the air with their fragrance. He didn't stop though, instead he wanted to show her the lake. That was where his soul was happiest in this hellish place.

They walked stone paths bathed in the golden light of the moon as well as a warm splash of color from the stained-glass lamps that lined the walkway. On occasion, Mia would stop to admire a plant and he would give a brief description before he encouraged her to move on. Finally, they reached the shores. The sound of water lapping at the land soothed his soul.

He dropped his arm and took Mia's warm hand in his. Locking their fingers together. "Come." They stepped to the edge of the water. The moon reflected off the surface like a giant globe.

"It's beautiful!"

"It gets even better. Hang on." He called on his power and transported them to a small island in the water's center. A gazebo covered with trailing white moonflowers stood tall and a spectacular view was had from the wooden swing hanging from its rafters.

"Wow. The moon seems to dance across the water. It's like

looking at a mirror." Surprisingly, she didn't pull her hand free from his. Instead, she turned to face him. Light played in the gray of her eyes, bringing forth a storm he wanted to drown in.

It was he who freed his hand. "I'm going to break your curse now. I need to touch you."

She gave a solid nod. "Okay."

He placed his palm just above her breasts and the rise and fall of her chest increased. His power flared, searched for the darkness in her soul, and when it was located, he pulled it free. "You are whole once again."

"Really?" She seemed to check herself. "I don't feel any different."

"Do you trust me?"

Mia searched his face. "I do."

The fact she trusted him was probably the greatest gift he had ever received. "Thank you." He led her to the swing where they both took a seat.

"Tell me about yourself. I mean other than what I already know," she said.

He stared over the rippling water. "I created this place as my escape from this world. Since I wasn't able to leave, I needed a place to go where I could clear my head." He cleared his throat. "There was a painful time in my life when I spent a lot of it here. I did things I am not proud of during that time."

"What happened?" She laid her hand on his arm.

"It is not something that should fall on your delicate ears."

"When my father left, I thought it was because I did something that drove him away. I did everything possible to please people after that, worried they would run off otherwise. When my brother died from a drug overdose, I actually contemplated taking my own life."

The thought of Mia and her beautiful soul stuck in eternal Hell made Hades shudder. "What made you change your mind?" It was obvious she still bore the scars of her brother's death.

"My mother needed me." Pain flashed in her eyes. "I wasn't

enough though. She took her life six months later." Her bottom lip trembled, and Hades sent out a quick command to his most trusted demon, Baal.

Find Mia's mother and be sure she is relocated. Tell Zarek that I will speak with him about it later.

Yes, my lord.

Hades had never asked Zarek for anything, but he would do this for Mia. He would make sure her mother's soul moved on to a better realm. He slipped his arm around her shoulders and pulled her close. "We cannot control those around us and certainly not the ones we love most. My own son, Drayos, was the one who placed a curse on the guardians. Blackened part of their soul so they would slowly become nothing but darkness and evil."

She tilted her head to look up at him. "Where is your son now?"

"Dead. He gave me a grandson, but as you know, Lowan is just as evil as his father. Apparently, my lineage is meant to be cursed in its own right." One of the reasons Hades chose to never father children again. "I also have a granddaughter, Lowan's sister whom I have allowed Lowan to imprison, Lileta who is the daughter of Lowan... Well, I cared for her no better." Never had he regretted his past more than now.

CHAPTER THIRTEEN

MIA MIGHT HAVE LOST her entire family but with the exception of her father, she knew they had loved her. There was no imagining the birth of an evil son or grandson. Hades had even been denied a loving family all the way to his own brothers. Perhaps being a deity was a worse fate than being human. At least she would eventually move on. It was in that moment her world came crashing down on her and she gasped, unable to believe it had not occurred to her earlier.

"My mother?"

"Is comfortable."

"I can't believe I didn't ask sooner. Can I see her?"

"Your mother is no longer in this realm. She has been moved."

"You did that. For me?"

"Yes."

She studied him. This man continued to surprise her as well as warm her heart. If he said her mother was safe, then she believed him. Mia brought her hand to his cheek, unable to comprehend he was the ruler of darkness when all she saw was a man who was lonely just like her.

"I cannot thank you enough." Before she realized what was happening, he leaned in and kissed her. Not a hungry one like he had done before, but soft and gentle before he pulled back.

"I am sorry. I vowed I wouldn't kiss you again, but your mouth was tempting me." He quickly grabbed her hand and helped her to her feet. Leading her closer to the water, she suddenly found a glass floor under their feet and it continued to appear in front of them as they walked farther out. Hades released her, and they were standing over the water, soft music filling the air.

"What's going on?"

Hades bent at the waist and bowed low. "May I have this dance, my lady?" He straightened and held his hand out. Bumps rose over her skin as she slipped her hand into his and he pulled her closer. Resting her free hand on his chest, they began to glide across the floor.

"Is there nothing you can't do?" She laughed. The evening was turning into the most magical night of her life.

"Nothing. Is there anything else you might desire?"

Mia grew heady from the floral fragrance filling the air as it mingled with Hades and his sinful scent. She felt almost drunk and was now bold enough to put her plan for the night into place. "Yes. There is."

"Name it. It shall be yours."

She pulled in a calming breath and let the words tumble from her tongue. "I want to spend the night with you."

He stopped suddenly, causing her to stumble into him. "Mia. I never thought to hear those words from you. Are you certain?"

"Positive."

"I want to ask why you changed your mind but don't want to question my good fortune."

She laughed. "I'll tell you anyway. I decided why not give in to the desire I feel? Now that my time here is almost near an end, I want you even more. I have grown fond of you, Hades."

"And I you." This time his kiss left gentle behind and was filled with desperation, passion, and fire. Every cell in her body tingled with pent-up desire.

His tongue stroked hers and sent an inferno roaring to life at her sex. She pressed into him, desperate to feel his naked body against hers but their clothes were in the way.

She swore under her breath.

Hades broke free, his own breathing as labored as hers. "Mia. You test my resolve to its limits."

"I don't mean to. Maybe we should forget dinner and move on to other things?" Lord knew her hunger wasn't for food. She wanted his hands all over her.

"That is the best idea I have heard all evening. We can always come back later. Or perhaps we can stay in my suite and dine."

"I love that idea." There was no going back now, nor did she want to. Once she had made up her mind to do something, there was no stopping her.

"Then to the palace." This time, rather than taking her hand or offering his arm, he pulled her into an embrace and swept her away. Moments later they arrived, and Mia found herself in Hades' room.

It was not at all what she expected. Rather than dark walls, they were pale yellow. The floors, a stark contrast to the rest of the palace and its high gloss marble, were a honey wooden plank. However, the king-size bed she spied in the other room was more in line with what she might expect the god of Hell to sleep in. Or do other activities. She experienced a rush of heat to her cheeks, followed by a tinge of jealousy when the thought of him and other women in that bed crossed her mind.

She locked it away. What Hades did was none of her business. She needed to live in the moment and enjoy it for what it was. A brief encounter with one damn sexy man.

"I find I can't wait to peel that dress away and reveal your luscious body beneath." Hades led her across the room and into the bedroom.

Mia could hardly wait as well. She was dying to see the man

beneath the clothes. There wasn't a doubt in her mind he was going to be spectacular. Plopping on the edge of the bed, she kicked off her heels. Relieved to be free of them. While she loved the shoes, heels were not something she was used to wearing. Rising back to her feet, she stepped into Hades and pushed her hands under his suit jacket. While he cut one fine specimen in a black suit and sapphire shirt, she wanted them gone. It also gave her an excuse to run her hands along the hard planes of his chest.

"Mia, I can scarcely believe you are here."

Neither could she. "I'm here, Hades. As real as you are." She slid the jacket over his shoulders and down powerful biceps until it fell to the floor. With trembling fingers, Mia worked the buttons on his shirt.

"You know I could simply use my power to remove these clothes."

She stared up at him. "And take all the fun out of undressing you?"

He grinned. "I was hoping you'd say that."

Smiling back, she continued on the buttons until the shirt was opened and fully revealed hardened muscle beneath. She pulled in a breath. Unable to believe she was finally able to lay her fingertips against his naked skin. After tracing invisible lines upward, his shirt followed the jacket. He stood before her with only his slacks which sat low on his hips. The dusting of dark hair that ran from his navel and dipped into his pants had her licking her lips. She was anxious to follow the path and see what she discovered at the other end.

"If you keep looking at me like you want to devour me, I'll forget my manners and tear that dress from your body," Hades growled.

Instant heat pooled at her sex and she met his fiery gaze. "When you talk to me like that..." She was unable to finish her train of thought.

He bent until his mouth touched her neck. A gentle kiss caressed her skin quickly followed by a scrape of his fangs. A sudden urge for him to sink the pearly points into her skin overwhelmed her. Everything about this man undid her.

Just as she was beginning to enjoy his mouth on her body, he stopped and took a small step back. His eyes were filled with molten desire as he grabbed the top of her dress and ripped, leaving her standing in only black lace panties.

HADES WAS FILLED with something he had never experienced in his entire existence. Raw smoldering desire for the woman standing in front of him. Sure, he had desired other females in his life. His sexual urges rivaled that of any male. Probably more so. But after centuries of the same ol', he had grown bored. His escapades less frequent and when he did share his body, it was simply to fuck until he was spent. That was not what he wanted now. Not with Mia. She was special, and he needed to remember that. Ripping her dress was probably not a wise choice but what was done was done.

"That was so unfair. I'm not able to tear your pants." She grinned letting him know she wasn't upset at his little escapade. Matter of fact, her musky scent filled the air around him, indicating just how aroused she was.

Before he could respond, she had freed his belt, unzipped his pants, and had them around his ankles. She dropped to her knees and wrapped long fingers around his throbbing shaft. His breath caught then slammed hard against his chest when she flicked out her tongue and tasted the tip of his cock.

"Damn," he moaned, lacing his fingers in her soft curls.

She sucked and pulled him into her mouth and his willpower nearly shattered. It took everything he had not to dig his nails into her scalp. Hurting her was not an option.

Ever.

Mia swirled her tongue around his head then began to move farther down his erection. She continued to work him until his knees went weak and he had to pull her away. "Mia..." He was barely able to speak. No woman had ever rattled him like this. "You need to stop before I lose total control." He lifted her to her feet and wrapped his mouth around her nipple. She arched into him with a moan on her lips. His hunger for her grew until he thought it would consume him. Lifting his head, he scooped Mia up and gently laid her on the bed where he kissed her. Devoured her mouth with such desperation he didn't think he would ever get enough.

The markings on his forearm tingled against his skin, indicating another soul had entered Hell. It was a stark reminder of who he was. What he was.

He was darkness. He was destruction and poison that would consume everything good. Hades was his father's son, and with that thought, memories Hades had kept locked away for centuries came back full force. Those of a god who had become so consumed by darkness, it had destroyed the one thing his father had loved more than anything.

His wife.

Hades' mother.

He broke free and sat up staring at Mia. She looked back at him, her lips swollen from his kiss. Desire in her stormy eyes and he knew what he had to do. There was no way he could allow this female to become sullied by his darkness.

"We can't do this."

Shock registered in her eyes. Quickly followed by hurt which had him removing himself from the bed. He jerked on his pants and cursed under his breath as he tried to pull the zipper over his erection.

"Did I do something wrong?" Her voice was low. Broken.

"No. You are perfect and that is why we cannot do this. I am darkness." He snapped his fingers making clothes appear over her nakedness. A sight he hated to cover. "You do not deserve my taint. Go home, Mia. Find a man who is deserving of you and forget I exist." On the last word, he sent her back to the mortal realm. His bed now empty and it was how it would stay. Hades would never enter this room again.

CHAPTER FOURTEEN

MIA STOOD in the middle of her small living room totally dumbfounded. Numb wouldn't even begin to describe how she was feeling. Rejected also came to mind, yet she had seen something in Hades' eyes.

Pain.

Suffering.

"Oh, Hades. I could never forget you exist." Nor did she want to. He was simply being silly, and she was going to make sure he understood that. She was an adult capable of making her own choices and she wanted him. Remembering she held his mark, she recalled the chant used before to summon him. Her palm heated. The tingling sensation spreading to her fingertips.

She waited.

Five minutes then fifteen went by. The clock indicated a half hour passed yet Hades hadn't shown. Mia rubbed her arms and began to pace. After a few minutes, she went to the kitchen and grabbed a bottle of water. Her thirst overwhelming or maybe it was simply something else to do. Realizing she didn't even know what day it was, she went in search of her cell phone. Finally, she located it on her nightstand and it told her the day was Friday, 4:00 am. Well, might as well get a shower because she had to be at work in a few hours.

Great. The bastard could have at least sent her home on a weekend. Trying not to feel rejected, she headed off to get ready for work.

An hour later, she was sucking back a cup of coffee and grabbing a jacket to head out the door. Her walk to the store was uneventful, and she even had time to swing by the abandoned buildings to check and see if Marion was still there. It didn't take long to locate the woman, and she quickly made her way closer to the campfire where Marion sat.

"How are things now that the demons are back?" She felt like she had been gone forever, but according to her phone it had only been a few hours.

The woman looked at her with tired eyes. "Even worse, but at least this area has been protected."

Mia frowned. "What do you mean protected?"

"The guardians formed some sort of protection around these buildings and the demons can't enter. I hear they did this in several locations while the demons were locked away."

"This is good then."

"It helps. They also bring in food, so we don't have to go out." Marion shrugged. "It's better than it used to be though not ideal."

Well at least this information made Mia feel better. She wondered what the rest of the world was like. "I'm glad to hear this. I'll check back later." She continued to make her way to the store and get things going. Normally, they were open twenty-four hours a day, but since the demon attacks, the store owners had decided it was safer to shut down at night. Mia had been happy since she normally would be coming in when it was still dark out.

HADES ADMINISTERED the newly condemned torture firsthand.

His mood so black everything around him turned to fire and brimstone. On his way back—he'd decided to walk rather than use his power to flash—he snarled at everyone he encountered. Anything that dared bloom, turn green, or look beautiful quickly began to decay as he made his way past. When he finally reached the gates of his palace, he spotted Baal on the other side.

"If you are here with bad news, I must warn you to keep it to yourself," Hades growled.

Baal lifted a brow. "Well, aren't you Mr. Fucking Sunshine. Your wrath can be felt all the way in the mortal realm."

Hades simply sneered and kept walking.

"You are smitten." Baal busted out into laughter. "The god of Hell has let a female get under his skin. Oh, how rich."

Hades whirled and swore steam escaped from his nostrils. "I warn you!"

Baal simply crossed his arms and leveled a glare on Hades. "If you torch me, you'll break Ranata's heart. I doubt you want her wrath."

Hades had been fighting Mia's summons all day. It had taken all his power along with a special spell to negate her call and keep him from automatically going to her. He had no idea how long he could keep it up, however. Hopefully, she would give up and stop calling. "I might be a monster, but I've no wish to hurt Ranata."

Baal snorted. "Well, I'm glad you like her more than me but seriously. Where is Mia? I heard a rumor that you sent her home."

"I did." Hades turned and began walking again.

"Why?" Baal stepped next to Hades. Apparently his number one demon wanted to drop a few notches on the list.

"I needn't answer you. In case you've forgotten, I'm in charge here."

"You're a cranky fuck. Just suck it up and whatever you did go apologize for it."

"I did nothing." Hades' reply was laced with venom. So much hate but it was only aimed at himself. How could he admit that he was not good enough for someone like Mia? She was innocence and light. He was something that would eventually tarnish her soul forever.

"Any news about my brother?" A change of subject was in order as they entered the front of the palace.

"Nothing so far."

He only responded with a grunt and continued with Baal on his heels trying to keep up.

"For fuck's sake, Hades. You going to light a fire or something?"

"What is it you want?" Hades stormed into his office and stopped in front of his desk. He tried to control his breathing and stop the incessant pounding in his temples. With a growl, he swiped his arm across his desk and sent everything crashing to the floor. The crystal glass shattered, and the laptop broke in half. He laid both palms on the wood surface and leaned forward. His temper was an entity of its own and right now it owned him. A pair of boots came into view to his right. He tilted his head to look up at his first officer, who stared at him with brows set high.

"Females can be vexing. They eat at our very souls and drive us to insanity. We can't breathe without them, and like the rest of us, you need to learn how to deal with it." Baal cleared his throat. "Now, care to tell Uncle Baal what the problem is?"

He finally straightened. "I sent her away because she does not deserve my taint. Mia deserves better than me."

"Well, welcome to the fucking club."

MIA ENDED her shift and began her walk home. She had half an hour before dusk began, and who knew what she would encounter on her way. Then Mia had caught up on the news while working. Lowan, apparently beyond irate that he had been locked down for a day, had destroyed several cities. Demons crawled from every crack and there were indications that in many areas they were coming out in broad daylight. She had no idea if those were a special demon, or if they had all become accustomed to the light. While Hell did have its own sun, it felt different from this one. She also remembered that Hades had the power to turn his world into whatever he wanted.

The thought of Hades. Those dreamy eyes. That sexy damn mouth and the way his tongue swiped across hers when he kissed sent ripples of desire over her skin. She still reeled from their earlier encounter, but something had stopped him. Mia had seen the turmoil in his eyes and it broke her heart. Deep down she knew he thought himself unworthy of her. Thought his darkness would eventually hurt her. Damn it, though, she was pissed that he didn't even bother to talk to her about it. Never gave her a chance to understand and tell him how she really felt. Instead he sent her away and now ignored her.

She wondered why the mark wasn't working to bring him back. Worry settled over her and made her muscles stiffen. Had something happened to him? He was a god and powerful, but was it possible that he could be injured? Maybe it was something so simple that he was somewhere he couldn't hear the summons. She really didn't have a full understanding of how it worked, and Hades had said his brother had invited him to rejoin the family. Perhaps he was there now. She hoped so because he deserved to have his family back. Still, she couldn't help missing him. Mia had grown fond of Hades. Probably too fond of the god and that alone worried her.

A few blocks away from her apartment building, she experienced a sudden searing pain in her gut. It was so extreme it caused her to double over. Mia rested her hand on the window ledge of the building next to her. Sweat trickled down her temples and she knew her stomach was going to reject all of its contents. Managing to make her way a little farther, she slipped into a narrow passage between two buildings, fell to her knees, and threw up. Shaking, she wiped her mouth and wished for a drink of water. Pain, like shards of glass being hacked into her back, ripped a cry from her lips. Her whole body trembled as she curled into a ball on the cold ground. Gravel dug into exposed skin, but she was too far gone to care.

"Dear god, someone help me." Her voice so low even she barely heard it. Certainly no one else would.

Black claws sprang from her fingertips and her skin felt as if it were on fire. Through the blur of her vision, she noticed patches of color on her arms. Something was terribly wrong, and deep down, she knew she was going to die.

Had Hades done something to her?

"Hades," she whispered before spiraling into the darkness.

THE DISTURBANCE SLITHERED across Lowan's skin like a seductive caress. He looked up from his desk and focused on Chaval, his Sumari warrior. The half-fae, half-demon male was a power to be reckoned with.

"Did you feel that?" Lowan asked.

Chaval stared straight at Lowan, his expression unreadable. "I did, my lord."

Lowan wondered why the warrior still remained faithful when he had no reason to be. Lowan had used Chaval's sister as leverage to force the warrior to do his bidding, but the guardian Lucan had managed to rescue Willow. Chaval insisted that he had a personal vendetta against the guardians and it was why he remained at Lowan's side.

Time would tell.

"Gather two of your men and we shall locate the power source. Quickly!"

Chaval gave a bow then disappeared only to reappear seconds later with two Wendigo demons. Within moments both men and the two demons were standing over a partially shifted female in the heart of New Orleans.

"Interesting." Chaval was the first to speak.

"Indeed," Lowan replied. He motioned to his demons. "Grab her and bring her back with us." While one of the demons hoisted the *thing* off the pavement, Lowan turned to Chaval.

"Have you ever seen anything like it before?"

Chaval seemed to contemplate for a moment before responding. "I've never seen it, but I have heard lore about it. It would seem the female is stuck mid-shift. Several things could be the cause, but this is likely her first attempt."

"That would make sense. Being human, she may not have even known what she was. The power, though, it is intoxicating."

"Yes. Lore suggests that the Arkoth demons were destroyed centuries ago due to the sweetness of their blood and the power one gains when they drink from them. This one may only now be coming into the age of transition. It's likely she had no idea who her father was. The DNA is buried so deep inside the females, no one can detect it. A self-preservation of sorts."

"I can hardly wait to taste her myself."

Lowan indicated it was time for them to leave. Once they were back to his hidey-hole in the middle of New Orleans, he directed his demons to place the creature in a room where he placed magical wards around it to prevent escape as well as a guard outside the door. With that deed done, he went in search of Chaval, so he could grill the fae for more information. The power the creature emitted had his mouth watering and his fangs pressing sharply against his lips. He wanted to be sure he took care not to kill her immediately.

CHAPTER FIFTEEN

HADES DECIDED the best thing to do was visit his home and be near his brothers, even though his grudge against Zarek was still as fresh today as it had been centuries ago. Truth be known, he needed to talk to Argathos. Words that his brother had uttered still rang in his mind. He knew damn well the seer was holding back and he intended to force the issue. There had to be answers as to why he felt like absolute shit and it was over a female. Something Hades had never given a care about in his entire life.

Summoning his power, he turned to Baal. "Hold down the fort, I'm going home."

"I thought you were home." The demon gave him a suspicious glare.

"Just fucking follow a command for once without your incessant backtalk." As power swirled around him, he heard Baal getting in the last word as usual. He made a mental note that when this was over, he would give the demon a job scrubbing the toilets. Nothing better than cleaning the bowels of Hell to give a demon new insight.

Moments later, he walked across the middle of his courtyard. Statues of gargoyles stood tall and guarded the archway into his home. From the outside, everything appeared as it had when his brother banned him eons ago. Hesitation kept him from entering the home he had not seen since he was a young god. His feet refused to move, yet he couldn't figure out why.

"You don't wish to enter without her." A voice carried on the breeze behind him. He didn't have to turn to know it was Argathos.

"As usual, I have no fucking idea what you mean."

His brother moved in beside him. "She frightens you. You fear your darkness will tarnish or maybe eventually hurt her."

He hated Argathos at this moment because he knew his brother to be right.

"Look how your love life turned out." He finally turned his focus on the god next to him. They were the same height and had once held the same eye color. For whatever reason, Hades' eyes had gone from deep brown to blue. "Look what happened to Zarek's own daughter. We are cursed."

"We also cannot live alone forever. It's a long damn time, Hades."

Hades snorted. "Tell me about it. Yet you have not found love again."

"I will. When the time is right." Argathos turned his attention back to the arching doorway that Hades simply could not walk through.

"What do I do when my darkness destroys her?" Hades already had his answer to that question. He would fall apart. In such a short time, that slip of a human female had burrowed under his skin.

"She is the one woman in existence who balances you. Another may not come along for centuries. Do you wish to wait?"

Hades scrubbed a hand over his whiskered face. "I should claim her then?" Hell, he had already marked her and hadn't removed his marking when he returned her to the mortal realm.

"Make your choice quickly or lose her forever. As we stand here discussing your love life, she is already in grave danger. Lower your barrier, brother."

His heart stuttered then stopped. Fear gripped him and cut off his air as he lowered the barrier he had placed to keep Mia from summoning him. Pain slammed him so hard it knocked him backwards. Once he realized what was happening, his fangs descended, and smoky clouds edged in black rolled across a clear sky.

Zarek appeared in front of them. "What the ever-loving hell?"

"His female is in danger." Thank goodness Argathos replied because Hades no longer had a voice. The blackness that resided inside him currently consumed his soul.

Hades swore there was a brief moment of sympathy in Zarek's eyes before they hardened. "Find your female, brother, but try not to destroy everything in your path in the process."

Hades wasted no more time as he summoned his power and split the very fabric of the temple of the gods. A gaping hole opened straight to Hell and Hades stepped through. He cared not one fucking iota if any of his demons leaked through to the other side. He was possessed. A demon in his own right with one exception.

His power was earth-shattering.

MIA'S HEAD pounded as if someone was hitting her with a sledgehammer. She tried to pry her eyes open but was met with sharp pain. Crying out, she steadied her breathing until the pain subsided some and tried again. She needed to know where she was. When finally she was able to open them a crack and peek around, her blurry vision picked up dark walls. It was obvious she was on a bed, but where? She searched her memories and barely recalled collapsing between two buildings in severe pain. Her stomach recoiling and hurling its entire contents on the ground. There had been something else too. She tried to remember but the headache was simply too much.

Pushing herself up ever so slowly, she waited for her stomach to rebel, but it didn't. Nor did her head ache any worse. She was finally able to take in the room around her. Next to her was a nightstand with what looked like a pitcher of water and an empty glass. Her throat screamed at her to do something about the razor blades she had apparently swallowed, so she carefully poured some water and took a sip. The coolness slid across her tongue and down her throat, bringing slight relief. Before she could set the glass down, the door to the room opened. Mia would recognize the black eyes filled with death anywhere. She tried to swallow the bitter taste of fear. The water threatened to speed back up her throat and land in her lap. "Where am I?"

The demigod who had created so much havoc in her world, as well as pressed a knife to her throat recently, crossed the floor with a lethal stride. "Imagine my surprise when I discovered a partially shifted female emitting an enormous amount of power right under my nose. Once I had you here, I quickly discovered I had my grandfather's mate at my mercy, and soon Hades will give me whatever I desire to get you back." He lifted a heavy shoulder and a grin that sent a cold shiver racing up her spine crept across his twisted mouth. "No, I won't be letting him have you."

He moved closer, stalking her, and she knew if she tried to bolt, he would show just what kind of lethal predator he truly was. She tried to reach for calm and find her voice. "I don't understand any of this. Shift into what?" She thought her curse was lifted. Had Hades not kept his word? A part of her didn't want to believe he would do that to her. As crazy as it sounded—and it was pretty insane—she had developed deep feelings for the god.

"And what do you mean by mate?" She understood the meaning behind it. There were women who had been human once, but they somehow had been fated to become the mates of a guardian. Now, they were part of the immortal world. Her pulse quickened. Was it possible she and Hades were meant to be together?

Lowan let loose a sinister laugh. "You, my dear, are a unique creature filled with unbelievable power and I intend to take it for myself. But not until I bring Hades to his knees." He entwined one of her curls in his fingers and she tried not to hurl.

"Hades marked you. It means he intends to claim you as his

mate." He laughed again. "Though I don't understand why he let you come back to the human realm. Apparently, he is in denial of what you are to him."

Well, so much for straight answers. Mia still had no idea what she was and even worse, how she was going to get out of this mess. The last thing she wanted was Hades stepping into a trap.

HADES NEARLY SHREDDED the universe when he ripped through it and entered Hell. When he stepped out mid-air, those near him dropped to their knees and quaked in their skin. His power rippled across the realm turning the sky black. Jagged lines of blood-red lightning threatened to shatter the sky above him. His temper never so foul in his entire existence. Finally, he had come to realize what Mia meant to him. Argathos had been trying to tell him in his own brotherly riddled fashion that Mia was Hades fated. He himself should have realized it when he'd marked her, yet he fed himself his own line of bullshit.

He still feared his darkness would snap her in half, but he had to trust things would work out. That is if he survived. The gods never revealed their secret. The one put into place long ago after their brother the Phoenix god was killed. They told everyone it was against their rules to harm another god or demigod. The fact of the matter was, they had put a power into place to prevent that from ever happening again. If they even tried to strike one of their own down, they would be met with instant death. It was the only way to protect themselves. However, Hades was almost willing to sacrifice himself in order to destroy Lowan. First thing he needed to do was procure the dagger stashed under a powerful spell in his palace. The only way to procure it was with eye recognition and a drop of his blood. It had seemed a good idea at the time, but now he was pissed he couldn't simply call the blade to him.

After flashing his way to his palace, he stormed across marble floors that cracked under his boots.

"Holy fucking hell!" Baal shouted behind him.

"Hades, what's going on?" Lileta, Baal's sister, was with him. Great, just what he fucking needed right at this moment.

"I'm going to kill Lowan," he snarled. Plaster crumbling off the wall.

"Damn. Lileta, I've never seen him like this. He's going to send this place to the ground, stone by stone." Baal spoke to his sister as if Hades wasn't even there.

Before Hades was able to cross the threshold to his office, Lileta placed herself in front of him, her golden eyes filled with power. She was the daughter of Lowan and a demigod in her own right. No one likely wanted to kill Lowan more than Lileta for all he had put her through. His grandson was the epitome of evil. A true spawn of the darkness and had he not messed with Hades' female, Hades might take a moment to appreciate such a calculated move.

"Out of my way."

She placed a hand on his chest. "You know the rules. You can't kill him." She lifted her chin slightly. "If not for the dire consequences to us, I would assist you in taking him down."

Hades rolled his fingers into tight fists and squeezed. "That piece of shit needs to learn a lesson." All the crystal lining the shelf in his office shattered on his words.

"Show him you mean business, but you can't kill him."

Hades was unable to breathe. "Lileta, you stand in my way." The last thing he wanted to do was hurt her, but he would forcibly move her from his path.

She glared at him but moved, nonetheless. Hades stormed to where he had the dagger hidden and barely registered the conversation behind him between Lileta and Baal. He did sense his first in command leave the palace. Now it was only Lileta.

"Mia would not want you giving your life for hers." Now the female was beside him.

"It's not a question of what she wants." This time, his favorite whiskey bottle shattered. Amber liquid dripped onto the carpet. One more thing to piss him off. He ignored it and touched the solid gold skull on the shelf, opening a secret cabinet where the eye scanner was located. As soon as he had scanned his right retina, an empty vile appeared. He bit down on his wrist and let the blood fill the container. Once that was completed, another door slid open and the dagger lifted through an opening in the bottom of the cabinet. The dagger, nested safely in black velvet, didn't look like something so valuable that it required such safekeeping defenses. Looks were deceiving. The steel blade would kill any immortal if stabbed in the heart. If used anywhere else on the body, it would make a wound that could eventually prove fatal. Before he was able to grab the dagger, a feminine hand touched his shoulder.

"Hades, please reconsider. Who will protect Mia once you're gone? I know you don't really want to leave her alone in the world."

Her words struck clear to the bone.

CHAPTER SIXTEEN

PANIC LACED with acid sat at the back of her throat and threatened to burn straight through her. What did Lowan intend for Hades? Mia imagined the piece of shit who towered over her wanted to take the god down.

"I thought there was some rule or something that said gods were not able to harm each other." She clearly recalled the explanation given to her by Hades earlier.

A grin curled his mouth into a twisted line of evil. "I don't need to touch him. You will be his downfall." He circled the room, a predator who enjoyed toying with his prey.

"Hades tossed me away. You said so yourself. It proves he doesn't want me, so what makes you think he will come for me?" She wasn't even sure herself that he would and secretly prayed he didn't.

Lowan lunged closer and ran a ringlet of her hair between his fingers. She held her breath. Fear prickling her skin as he produced a knife. Before she could blink, he sliced off the curl. "Hades will go mad when he receives this." He held the piece of hair up and it vanished. Another mystical currier on its way to Hades. Might even be in his hand this very second. Mia held no real understanding of how the paranormal world around her worked, but it was both a wondrous and scary place.

She had hoped after taking a piece of her hair, Lowan would leave her alone, but it was not to be. This time he grabbed a handful of hair, jerked her head to the side, and pain so intense had her crying out as he struck her neck with thick, sharp fangs. Intense burning followed the vein in her neck, down her right arm and to her fingertips where it shot across her stomach and burned her intestines. Mia tried to fight. Wanted to shove him away but found herself paralyzed. As dots of color danced in her vision, something deep inside her burst forth. Black claws sprung from her fingertips and she swiped at his cheek. Lowan snarled and shoved her away. His fangs tearing the flesh on her neck, warm wetness trickled across her skin. She managed to glance down at herself and noticed her skin appeared to glow. What was happening to her? It was nothing like the shift she had made nightly into a spirit. This was different. She was energized, as if plugged into an electrical outlet. There was also no missing the sharp points that stabbed her bottom lip.

She had freaking fangs!

"You'll pay for that, bitch!" Lowan unleashed a current of power that streaked across the room and wrapped a blanket of pain over her entire body. Every muscle went rigid until she convulsed. When he finally released his magical hold, she collapsed into a trembling mass onto the floor.

"You cannot beat me." Thankfully, he left the room and she curled into a fetal position on the cold stone floor.

HIS ENTIRE BODY went rigid when a lock of Mia's hair appeared in his palm quickly followed by blinding pain. For a moment, Hades was unable to move. Not understanding what was happening until dawning struck like a bolt of lightning.

"Hades? What's wrong?" Concern etched lines on Lileta's forehead.

"He's hurting her. That fucking little prick is making Mia suffer." Electrical current sizzled in the air and every piece of furniture splintered. The very atmosphere of Hell fractured. As Hades began his shift, Lileta took several steps back, her eyes wide. It was rare that anyone bore witness to his darkest side. The side that was all his father. A creature whose eyes burned with Hell's fire. Whose skin darkened to black and leathery wings unfurled from his back as his clothing shredded from his body that had grown several inches taller.

"Damn, I think you need to get ahold of yourself, Hades."

There was no stopping his craze. Denial of what Mia was to him no longer a valid excuse. Her pain tore a hole in his heart that he swore would never heal. With a snarl on his lips, he vanished from the room leaving the dagger behind. Lileta was right, he would do Mia no good if he were dead. He trusted only himself to protect her. The thought of another man touching her, looking at her, fueled him further.

It only took minutes for Hades to locate Lowan's fortress on the outskirts of New Orleans. The power that surrounded the old plantation held the signature of the demigod. If Lowan thought to keep Hades out with such pitiful magic, his grandson was a disgrace to everything evil. Even the darkness mocked him and his attempts at world domination. Sure, Lowan currently rained terror in the human realm, but any lackey could terrorize mortals. Hell, Hades' own demons were known to raise havoc on many occasions throughout the centuries.

Within seconds several demons descended. Some from the air, many poured from the structure itself, and several ripped through the earth. Hades' laughter became maniacal as he slaughtered some and sent many back to Hell with no escape. Those who dared commit treason against him would join the shadow demon he had locked away. The one awaiting centuries of torture Hades would mete out for threatening Mia.

The ground shook and fractured as Hades' power collided with Lowan's and his hundreds of demons. Even the sun hid behind black clouds, turning the sky a dismal gray. Fortunately, Lowan's fortress was in the middle of a swamp and not close to the city's center. That didn't mean there would be no repercussions, however. Any in the immediate vicinity would experience the ripple of power. That's why when the guardians showed up—no doubt feeling the power themselves—Hades dispatched them to keep the wider impact to a minimum. It was the least he could do.

Baal appeared next to him as well as one hundred demons under his command. "Ready to kick some ass, boss."

Hades grinned. Baal was his right hand and often a cocky rebel, but when things got dirty, the demon was as loyal as any Hades had ever known. "Then let us tear this place to the ground, but keep in mind Mia is my number one priority." On his last word, Hades let his power rip free and flashed himself inside the fortress.

Once inside, he was immediately met by Lowan. "Grandfather. How kind of you to oblige me and step right into my trap." It was then Lowan's Wendigos rushed forward. Hades rolled his eyes. The creatures had never been very bright, following whoever would lead them. Apparently, they had forgotten who they were dealing with.

With a sweep of his arm through the air, Hades took down the first wave of fifty pitiful demons. Dropping them into lifeless clumps of goo. The next round took a step forward and Hades issued his warning.

"Are you that fucking daft? If you wish to die, then I will end you all now. I've no time to waste." In seconds, the battlefield cleared of all Lowan's henchmen. Apparently, they weren't as dumb as Hades thought. With Baal and his army behind him, Hades issued his last warning as he faced Lowan.

"Step aside. Allow me to take Mia from here and you can continue your terror on humanity."

"If I don't?" Lowan puffed out his chest and straightened but was still shorter than Hades' beast.

"You silly fool. What you do in this world is of little concern to me. However, when you fuck with what is mine. Dare to even look at or speak her name, then you have crossed a line." Without hesitation, Hades flicked his wrist and sent a thousand Brones demons coursing through Lowan's bloodstream. Tiny creatures of Hades' own creation that would bore into every cell in his grandson's body. The demigod's intestines would feel like they were being drilled by shards of glass in… One. Two… and down Lowan went. Into a fetal position, he writhed in pain as he looked up at Hades.

"You…" He couldn't speak as the demons shredded his voice box.

"You will not die but will beg for death. Eventually, you will figure out how to rid yourself of them. In the meantime, they will consume your insides and every time you regenerate the torture will start anew." He stepped closer, glared down at his own flesh and blood. "I am Hades, god of the Underworld and you can never best me. If you ever touch Mia again, I will kill you and damn the consequences." Then he stormed off to collect his mate.

MIA WOKE to the floor under her shaking and the bed frame screeching across the stones. She quickly pushed herself up, her head still filled with a fog from whatever Lowan had done to her. Thankfully, he was nowhere to be found. She managed to get to her feet and noticed her skin still held the same glow it had before. Renewed energy filled her with determination. She was going to get out of here and whatever was going on outside her room would make a good distraction. As she crossed to the door, she spotted her reflection in a mirror and came to an abrupt halt. Stepping closer, she was hardly able to comprehend what stared back at her.

Small horns protruded from the top of her head. Her ears now had pointed tips and her skin was a luminescent bronze. Even her eyes appeared brighter than she'd ever seen. She curled her lips to reveal the small set of fangs she had felt pressed against her tongue.

What the hell had Hades done to her?

As soon as her mind posed the question, the door to her prison blew off the hinges and seven feet of pissed off demon stormed through. The beast stopped short and stared at her and there wasn't any doubt in her mind that it was Hades. Anger fueled her next move as she instinctively raised her hand and launched a burst of power at him. He deflected and right before her eyes transformed from the dark beast back to the sexy man she knew. Seeing the handsome god made her heart ache even more. He had abandoned her but not before he turned her into whatever that was that had stared back at her in the mirror.

"Mia—"

"How could you?" she shouted, cutting him off. "I trusted you to keep your word." She curled claw-tipped fingers into her palms, drawing blood. His nostrils flared as he looked down at her bleeding hands.

He stormed toward her. She took a step back as a loud blast rocked the ground and caused her to stumble. Hades was there to catch her. Press her against his hard body and she hated him even more for the desire that bloomed deep in her soul. A desire that was only for him.

"I am truly sorry, but I must get you to safety and then we will talk."

She beat her fist against his chest. "Look what you did to me!"

He only squeezed her tighter to him. "I swear I did not do this to you. At least not intentionally, but I will get to the bottom of it." Another explosion. "We must leave. My army is busy destroying this place."

Before she was able to respond, the room went black and she knew they were sucked into a vortex. Well, fine with her. Mia could hardly wait to give Hades a piece of her mind and maybe even her fist across his damn kissable lips.

MIA WAS LIKE HEAVEN AGAINST HADES' body and he had never been more relieved. The first thing he was going to do was get her back into his bed and finish what had been started. He was such an idiot for ever letting her go in the first place. He also would be finding out how his female had suddenly become an Arkoth demon. He would ask Lileta to research the vast library, but he was positive he knew the answer.

Flashing into his suite, he reluctantly set Mia on her feet. Hating to let her go but knowing she would need some distance and an explanation. He would never be able to apologize enough.

She shoved away from him. "Well, I suppose I should thank you for saving me, but if not for you I probably wouldn't have been in that predicament," she spat.

"You are correct. I should have never let you go, and I don't intend to make that same mistake again." He stepped closer, unable to keep his distance.

She backed up. "Stay away from me." Her skin glowed the closer he got, and her musky arousal filled the air.

"I am sorry, Mia." Hades did something he had only ever done once in his entire existence and that was when he had pledged his allegiance to his brother, Zarek. He dropped to one knee, took her hand in his, and stared into her stormy eyes. "I vow to never turn you away again. I vow to be your protector, provider, and lover for eternity. I, Hades, god of the Underworld, have finally found my other half. I love you, Mia, and want you to become mine."

She gasped.

He held his breath and waited for her rejection. Lord knew he deserved it as he was an absolute beast.

"I should be furious with you, yet I understand what you did." She knelt in front of him and touched his face. "You only meant to protect me from your darker side. Promise me you'll never fear that side of yourself again."

He did not deserve this kind, loving female. "I will do anything for you. Even if it means leashing the beast that lives inside me."

She shook her head. "No. Never hide who you really are from me. I love all of you, Hades."

Relief swept over him. She loved him as well. Everything would be right in his world now.

"Now, are we going to finish what we started?" Her brow arched as she glanced at the bed.

CHAPTER SEVENTEEN

MIA HARDLY BELIEVED A GOD--AND not simply any god, but freaking Hades—was on his knees declaring his feelings. The moment was almost surreal. When she glanced at her skin, she noted she was back to normal. Was it because of Hades? So many questions, but right now all she could think about was taking care of their unfinished business. Getting him naked and back into that bed. Maybe she'd keep him there for a week. He must have read her mind because he grinned and this time she didn't care if he knew her thoughts.

Hades jumped to his feet, pulling her with him, and with a snap of his fingers, they were both naked. "Didn't want to waste any time."

"I'm glad. I would be more than happy to strip you later. Right now, I want your hands all over me." She stepped backward in the direction of the bed.

He stalked. The look of a predator in his eyes and she swore she was going to melt into a puddle right there on the floor. Instead, she kept moving back, liking the game of pursuit.

"My hands and my mouth will be all over you, Mia. I will never have enough of you." He finally reached her and slipped his arms around her waist, pulling her close. Before he could go any further, she planted her palms on his chest.

"I need to know that I'm all you desire. That there will be no more women." She held her breath. Hades was well known for his womanizing ways. She had heard the talk while she was here.

"There will never be another woman. You are it for me. This, I also vow."

It was all she needed to hear. She slipped her arms around his neck and kissed him. Poured everything she was feeling into the kiss, so he would realize how deeply she felt. It surprised her how quickly she had fallen for Hades, yet it felt so natural. It was right that they were together and now she knew she'd been waiting for him her entire life.

Hades ended the kiss and dipped his head. Ran his tongue around the edge of her nipple. Teasing. Tormenting, until she wanted to beg him for more. When she arched back and leaned into him, he finally got the idea and pulled the pulsing tip into his mouth.

"That feels so good," she whispered.

He stopped long enough to lift his hungry gaze to hers. "I intend to make you feel more than simply good."

She shivered. Knowing he was going to keep his word as he moved to the other breast and gave it his special attention. Before she could pull her thoughts together, he lifted her and carried her to the bed where he laid her on the softest linens her skin had ever touched.

"I feel like I've waited forever to touch you, Mia."

The feeling was certainly mutual and when he began to lick and kiss his way down her stomach, both hands cupping a breast, she moaned. He rolled her nipples between his fingers, giving a hard pinch before he slid his hands along her waist and settled them on her hips. Hot breath caressed her skin and tickled the hair on her inner thigh as he placed a gentle kiss.

She sank her fingers into his hair and tried to encourage him to move to her core, but he only chuckled.

"I plan to torture you until you are begging me to take you."

She groaned. "You are a beast."

He suckled the flesh so close to her sex, she thought she might orgasm from the sheer pleasure of it. A swipe of his tongue along her channel and up to her nub had her digging nails into his scalp and thrusting her hips upward. Rather than give her what she so desperately desired, he planted light kisses on her other thigh.

"Hades," she whispered.

"Mia, your taste is the sweetest nectar. I don't think I will ever get enough." And to prove his point, he swirled his tongue across her clit and slid a finger deep inside her.

This time she fisted his hair. "More."

He obliged by sucking her nub into his mouth, a fang scraped across her bundle of nerves causing her to shatter into oblivion.

MIA'S RELEASE danced across Hades tongue and made his already stiff cock even harder. He'd not thought it possible, yet it appeared it was. All he could think about was sinking deep inside her. Both his cock and his fangs. He slid up her body, kissing her soft flesh as he went until he was settled with the tip of his shaft at her apex. He caught her gaze.

"I want all of you, Mia. I need to taste your blood. I need to make you mine." He waited for her to recoil, but instead she smiled and turned her head exposing her slender neck to him.

"I want to give all of myself to you. I want to be yours."

Her words only encouraged him to thrust into her until he was fully seated. Both of them groaned. He kissed her neck. Suckling the flesh until he couldn't stand it another second. With lightning speed, he sank his fangs until blood filled his mouth and he took two small pulls before he retracted them and sealed the puncture. He didn't want to claim her just yet.

She kissed his jaw as he moved his hips, thrusting into her silky wetness. He had to remember to breathe when she tightened her grip around his shaft. Otherwise, he was going to lose total control of himself and he wanted their first time together to be gentle.

Lowering his head, he latched onto a nipple and pulled it into his mouth. He swirled his tongue over the rosy bud, eliciting a moan from her as her hips met his.

"Faster," she pleaded.

Hades leaned back, gripped her thighs, and parted her legs farther as he gave her what she begged for. The desire in her eyes as she gazed at him stroked his ego. He had put that there and when she finally cried out, her orgasm ripping through them both, he allowed his own release to take over. After several moments of holding her close, he rolled off but kept his hold on her, pulling her to him.

"That was amazing," she practically purred.

"I'm nowhere near done with you. I intend to fully claim you as mine."

"Didn't you already mark me?" She traced lazy circles on his chest with her fingers.

"I did and I'm afraid that mark is what awakened the Arkoth inside you."

She raised her head to look at him, brows arched. "Arkoth?"

"Yes. Their species is rare. They hold a power that others crave to take, therefore most have been wiped out by greedy blood suckers."

Mia pushed herself up and Hades moaned at seeing her exposed breasts. "I'm not following. How could I be one of these creatures. I'm human."

"I'm afraid your father was not."

"My father?"

He reached up and brushed a curl from her cheek. "I have my best trackers on him now." Lileta had already reported in that she was close to locating Mia's father. "I surmise your father remained hidden in order to protect you. Eventually, a male Arkoth reaches the age where he can no longer hide what he is. This would attract others to him and therefore bring danger to his children."

MIA LET the words sink in but still couldn't comprehend them. Her father was a demon? Anger filled her. "My brother would have been half demon as well?" This might explain why Danny had so much difficulty that had led to his overdose. Her father was a coward who left them to deal with something they couldn't understand.

"No. It appears your brother did not have the same father as you."

Mia jumped from the bed, pulling the covers with her. "Are you saying my mother cheated on my father?" It was something she couldn't even begin to wrap her head around.

"No. I'm saying that man who left you as a child was not *your* father. He was your brother's."

She had to sit. Plopped into a chair and leaned into the cool leather. "This is a lot to take in." Hades was kneeling in front of her. Taking her hands into his.

"Love, I promise I will find your father and hopefully get answers to at least some of your questions."

She couldn't help but smile. In spite of everything, she was lucky to have found—or, in this case been found by—Hades. The sexiest, most powerful man to exist wanted her as his own. "Tell me, how does this mating thing work between us?"

A grin only Hades could wear curled his lips. "I'm afraid it requires us going back to bed."

She reached out and fingered his dark hair. Brushing it across his forehead. "Hmm. That sounds delightful. What else?"

"We must exchange blood for the bond to form completely."

The thought of drinking blood should horrify her. However, it totally turned her on. Even caused an ache deep in her gums as her small fangs started to grow. Suddenly, the pulse that beat in his neck called her and it was all she could think about. "This whole demon thing. Will I ever have control over it?"

"Yes, and especially once you share my power. I will help you every step of the way." He rose then bent and scooped her from the chair. Carrying her back to the bed, she noticed something pass in his eyes as the covers she'd been holding fell to the floor and left her naked in his arms.

"Do you trust me, Mia?" he whispered as he lay her down.

"Yes. Whatever it is you are thinking of doing to me, I trust you completely." Heat flared in her sex when his pupils dilated. She could hardly wait to see what he had in store. She glanced down and noticed he was fully erect again.

She licked her lips, desperate to taste him. Bring him the same pleasure he had given her. Instead, Hades kissed her as he gripped her wrists and slid her arms over her head, pinning her under him. His tongue delved and consumed every inch of her mouth, yet Hades demanded more. Just when she thought she could no longer stand the aching between her thighs, he slipped inside her and she took every thick inch of him. Swearing she was going to come undone with each stroke. He broke the kiss and she was left shaken.

"Mia. You must take my blood." Before she could even ask how, he bit his wrist and held it out to her. Rather than be repulsed, she latched onto him and drank as if her very life was at stake.

Power, pure and raw, coursed through her veins. How she knew this, Mia was uncertain, yet she realized the energy she experienced was different from what she had pulled up earlier to fight against Lowan. After several more pulls, she released her grip on his arm. Hades' puncture wound healed right before her eyes.

He nuzzled her neck then the bite came. Different from the one earlier, this one sent a tingle straight to her nub, and with each pull he took, pleasure rocked her world. Mia drifted on a sea of bliss, experiencing one orgasm after another. It was almost too much to bear. After what seemed an eternity, Hades retracted his fangs and reached his own release, taking Mia with him once again.

Something shifted inside her and she was suddenly flooded with emotions not her own. They overwhelmed her and then they were gone.

"Sorry. I wasn't expecting the connection to be instantaneous."

"Those were your emotions?" She ran her fingers along his jaw, enjoying the soft whiskers on her skin.

"Yes. We are now bonded. I will feel what you feel and vice versa unless we block each other. We should even be able to communicate telepathically."

Simply amazing.

Yes, it is.

Mia stared at him before opening her mouth. "Wow. That was unreal."

He grinned then pulled free from her. "There will be a lot of unreal moments. For now, your father has been located and is being brought here. We should dress."

There were no words to describe the turmoil that rolled in her gut. She was going to meet her real father. A man she hadn't even known existed until today.

CHAPTER EIGHTEEN

HADES WAS DRESSED and storming down the corridor within minutes of receiving the message from Baal that Mia's father had been located. He had insisted on meeting the demon before Mia got anywhere near him. Reluctantly, she had agreed and was waiting in their suite with Baal's mate, Ranata. Hades was certain the only reason Mia was being so cooperative was because she didn't want to offend the fae queen and this was their first meeting. He hoped the females got along. He wanted Mia to have friends as well as allies in this new world of hers.

He shoved open the door to his office and stepped inside. The demon next to Baal dropped to one knee.

"My lord."

Hades didn't indicate for him to rise, instead he studied the man. Same dark hair and coffee-colored skin as Mia. "Look at me," he commanded.

The demon tipped his head back and stared at Hades with the same gray eyes Hades had looked into earlier. He had to give credit. The man didn't show any fear and that was something Hades could respect.

"You may rise."

The demon stood to his full height, which matched that of Hades' six-foot-three and didn't once cast his gaze downward. A sign that while he respected Hades' position, he was also a warrior who would not be intimidated.

"What is your name?"

"Omar."

"You have been summoned here regarding your daughter." No sense beating around the bush. He watched for any indications of how this demon felt regarding the matter. Omar's features remained unchanged.

"My daughter?"

"Yes. Certainly, you have felt her power."

"I thought I had but it was so brief and never returned I thought I had imagined it. You know of my daughter? Is she well?" There was a glimmer of hope in his eyes.

"She is, but you will need to be explaining the situation to her. You can understand that she is confused."

Omar gave a single nod. "Yes. Where can I find her?"

"She is here, and you should also know that Mia is now my mate. You hurt her, and you pay the penalty. I promise it will be one that will last for an eternity."

The demon's gaze softened. "I am honored to have you mated to my only daughter. Please, I am anxious to see her."

Hades tipped his head. "Then it shall be done."

MIA WAS ENJOYING her chat with Ranata. The fae queen turned out to be no different from Mia herself. Seems both their lives were a total mess. Ranata, however, was only beginning to find out just how messed up hers was and Mia wouldn't want to trade places for anything. Finding out you were queen to an entire race of people definitely didn't sound like good times.

"I can't believe you and Hades. We didn't even get a chance to throw you a party! That will be rectified and soon."

Mia offered a smile. Still not used to the fact that she was now basically the wife of the god of the Underworld. Un-freaking believable!

Mia.

She jumped, not used to Hades entering her mind. *What?*

Are you ready to meet your father?

Panic must have caused lines on her face because Ranata gave her a funny look.

"Are you okay?"

"Yes. I'm just not used to this non-verbal form of communication. Also, Hades asked if I was ready to meet my father." Her body shook from the emotions that racked her.

"Are you? It is a big step. I remember how nervous I was when I saw my mother again."

Mia recalled the story Ranata had shared earlier how her mate, Baal, had bargained with Zarek in order for Ranata to see her mother in the afterlife. Miracles never ceased, and she wondered if she might one day see her own mother again. Pulling her shoulders back, she replied.

Hades, I'm ready. I'll be there in a moment. Mia looked at Ranata. "Walk with me?" She knew the woman would offer much needed moral support.

"I'm so happy you want me to accompany you." Ranata laced her arm around Mia's and led her out of the room. As they walked down the corridor that seemed to go on forever, Mia tried to calm her nerves. It was unreal that she was going to meet her father. A demon.

As they approached Hades' office, he stepped out and greeted her with a kiss on the cheek. "Your father is a good man and is anxious to see you." He offered his arm to Mia and a warm smile to Ranata then escorted both of them inside.

A man as tall as Hades, with a head of black hair and the same eyes that Mia stared at every time she looked in the mirror, met her gaze. There was no mistaking he was her father, and if his looks weren't enough, she felt it deep in her soul.

He took several steps toward her then stopped. "You are as beautiful as your mother."

Suddenly she needed to know everything. "How did you come to be with my mother, impregnate her, and then leave?" Surprisingly, there was no anger in her regarding the situation.

Sadness drew lines across his face. "I met your mother through a mutual friend and there was an instant attraction. I never hid what I was from her. She knew and had even seen me in my demon form. She was the most accepting woman I had ever met." He glanced at the floor, no longer did he look like a formidable warrior. More like a broken man and Mia took the last few steps. Reaching him, she placed her hand on his arm.

"What happened?" she asked in a gentle tone.

He looked her in the eyes. "She became pregnant. It wasn't supposed to happen, but the gods must have willed it so. I knew I had to leave her to keep you both safe. I prayed your power would never surface." He gently gripped both her arms. "There was a real good chance it wouldn't, and you would be safe." He looked over her shoulder at Hades. "I never imagined you would become the mate to the most powerful god ever. I am pleased he will be your protector."

Mia pulled her father into an embrace. "I understand." And she really did. There was a kind of connection with this man that told her he spoke only the truth.

He squeezed her, kissing the top of her head. "I am the luckiest man alive. I will assist you in your transition and make sure you know how to use your power." He released her, and Hades came in beside her.

"That makes two of us. You will have an entire army to protect you as well. Nothing and no one will dare harm you again."

HADES HAD INSISTED Omar stay in the palace and already placed the demon in a suite of his own. He was welcome here for as long as he wanted to stay. Hades liked the fact there was another he could trust to care for Mia besides himself and Baal. There was still the little incident with Lowan, but he hoped the little prick would take care before he fucked with Mia again.

After checking in with Argathos, he learned there was still no news of Aidyn returning. However, both of his brothers were anxious to meet their new sister-in-law and Hades couldn't agree more that Mia would be far safer in the gods' realm than in Hell. At least until her power was fully under her control. He currently made his way to find his lovely bride and tell her they were going to move. At least temporarily. He located her in the kitchen, supervising the cook.

"Love." He wrapped his arms around her waist, causing her to turn into him. Her smile undid him. Gods, how had he fallen so hard for this female? It didn't matter. A question he could not answer, nor did he care to.

"You look like you're up to something." She smiled.

"Yes. We are going to be making a temporary move to my other home."

"You mean where your brothers live?"

"Yes. It will be a safer place for you while you learn your powers. Besides, my brothers wish to meet you, and there are many who can also help you as well as provide protection."

"What about my father?"

"He will come as my guest. Zarek will not dare tell me who I can have in my home."

"Okay. When do we leave?"

"Start packing anything you want to take with you. We will leave as soon as you're ready. Just remember, I can get you anything you desire. Soon, you'll be able to do the same."

"So, pack light?" She laughed as she walked away toward their suite.

An hour later, and they were settled into a home he had not been in since he was exiled to Hell. Nothing had changed. Everything in its place as it had been so long ago. Everyone was in their rooms and he lay with Mia in his arms.

"It was so nice meeting Zarek, Qadira, and Argathos today. I can't wait for the party tomorrow, so I can meet the others." She snuggled in closer. "I know I'm going to like everyone, and it really is a comfort having so much support." She kissed him on the cheek. "Thanks for bringing my father along. We both have a lot of time to make up for."

He rolled on top of her. Pinned her arms over her head and nuzzled her neck. "Anything to make you happy."

"Ohh. Right now, this makes me happy," she purred.

Hades would do anything to make this woman smile. "I love you and I intend to devote my entire existence to showing you just how much."

So many things were wrong in the world, but finally it seemed fate had smiled on him. Mia was a strong woman, a rare demon who would only grow her power every day. Together, they could do anything, and he couldn't wait to get started.

PAIN SLICED through his chest and squeezed his heart. An invisible grip wrapped around the organ so tightly that he clenched his jaw. Fangs punched through his bottom lip as his entire body convulsed. Muscles locked down and kept him pinned to where he lay. Aidyn's mind a mess of jumbled memories that were familiar yet felt as if they belonged to someone else. There was one that shouted above all the rest of a raven-haired beauty.

Tears filled her blue eyes then fell to caress her cheek. Full lips folded inward between her teeth as she bit down on the soft flesh and stared back at him.

Her pain gutted him.

He wanted to pull her to him and kiss her mouth. Ease her heartache and then he would slay whatever had caused her so much grief. His feelings for her confused him. He didn't even know her name.

A wall of flames licked all around him, but their heat never touched his skin. Oddly, he was cold. So very cold and alone. He screamed until his throat was raw and he swore his intestines were being shredded. Something inside him clawed to be free.

Where was he?

All he could see was the wall of flames. If he stared long enough, she came to him again. Who was the beautiful female that refused to go away? Deep down he knew she was the cause of his pain.

The flash of a blade in her hand as she came toward him.

He should wish her to suffer as he did, yet the very idea of it made him hurt worse. More memories. Pictures of a war centuries old flashed behind his closed eyes.

Hundreds of bodies cold on a battlefield and three men stood next to him.

He realized they were powerful beings the same as him. Brothers? His soul recognized them to be men he cared deeply for. Where were they now? Why did they not come to his aid? Maybe they were being tortured as well. A powerful instinct to protect them and the unknown female pushed him to force his body into cooperation. Aidyn commanded constricted muscles to relax enough that he was able to rise to sitting. The flames dropped slightly so he could focus his blurry vision on his surroundings. Besides the fire, there were two torches casting shadows on stone walls that boxed him into a small room. No windows and no exit as far as he could tell. He sucked in a ragged breath, wishing he knew where the fuck he was and why he hurt so damn bad. Another vision slammed into him.

The female with eyes the color of sapphires shoved a blade into his chest.

He clawed at his own flesh to try to stop the pain. Knowing she had tried to kill him didn't bring rise to his anger, only a drive to find her and assure himself she was safe. Looking at his chest, he was surprised to see blood dripping from a wound that he swore hadn't been there earlier. Apparently, he was losing his mind. Nothing made sense as he rolled off the stone slab and through parted red-orange flames to land with a hard thud on his knees.

His gut twisted as nausea threatened to send his stomach into a convulsing fit. He ignored it and crawled—the naked flesh on his knees scraping against hard stone left a trail of blood as he went. There had to be a way out. Instinct drove him until he reached the wall where he clawed his way to his feet. Taking a moment to rest, he placed his forehead on the stone, absorbing the coolness while he waited for the dizziness to pass. He'd gone from freezing to sweating in a matter of seconds.

After what seemed an eternity, he began to pull himself along the wall. He searched for something but had no idea what until he located it.

A small crevice.

He slipped his fingers inside. Stone tearing at his knuckles but he ignored the pain. What he sought was here and it struck him as odd, considering he had no idea where he was. Finally, his fingertips brushed across what felt like a lever. He pressed it and the ground shook as the wall next to him slid open. Cool, fresh air rushed in and Aidyn managed to make his way outside where the passage opened to a large room. Squinting against the brightness, he spotted a statue. Seven feet of golden metal in the form of a man stood across the room. The wings at his back were spread wide. The face was partially covered by a mask, a small pair of jeweled wings jetted from either side to create a glorious crown.

"Impressive, isn't it?" a voice called out.

He swung his gaze to focus on the individual who sat on the throne beside the statue. "Who are you?" Razors sliced at his throat.

"I'm hurt that you do not remember me, Uncle." The man rose, his height only slightly less than Aidyn's own. "I am Lowan and I've come to care for you while you recover."

Finally, relief swept over him that family was here to assist him until he regained his strength. "I am in your debt, nephew."

The man offered a smile. "Think nothing of it."

ABOUT THE AUTHOR

Award winning and bestselling author Valerie Twombly grew up watching Dark Shadows over her mother's shoulder, and from there her love of the fanged creatures blossomed. Today, Valerie has decided to take her darker, sensual side and put it to paper. When she is not busy creating a world full of steamy, hot men and strong, seductive women, she juggles her time between a full-time job, hubby and her German shepherd dog, in Northern IL. Valerie is a member of Romance Writers of America and Fantasy, Futuristic and Paranormal Romance Writers.

Sign up for Valerie's newsletter and be the first to hear about new releases, receive special excerpts and exclusive contests. http://valerietwombly.com/newsletter-sign/

Follow Valerie
www.valerietwombly.com

facebook.com/fangedfantasy

twitter.com/fangedfantasy

instagram.com/valerietwomblyauthor

ALSO BY VALERIE TWOMBLY

Visit ValerieTwombly.Com

Guardians Series

Vampire's Mate Book 1

Dragon's Fate Book 2

Vampire's Kiss Book 3

Demon's Destiny Book 4

Hades Book 5

Vampire's Queen Book 6

Vampire's Desire Book 7

Eternally Mated Series

An Angel's Torment Prequel

Fall Into Darkness Book 1

Veiled In Darkness Book 2

Bound By Darkness Book 3

Unleash The Darkness Book 4

Surrender To Darkness Book 5

Tempted By Darkness Book 6

Sparks Of Desire Series

His Burning Desire

Rescue Me

Finding Hope

Demonic Desires Series

Taken By Desire Book 1

Taken By Storm Book 2

Jinn's Seductions Series

Spanish Nights

Sultry Nights

Beyond The Mist Series

Passion Awakened (Beyond The Mist)